MICHAEL'S SOUL MATE

Vampires of London Book 2

LORELEI MOONE

CONTENTS

CHAPTER ONE

Michael checked his watch and scanned the room. Little groups of people stood scattered around the tastefully lit hotel lobby, drinks in hand. Some were making small talk, others had paired up to dance toward the other end of the establishment, beyond the bar. Some had even left, no doubt to take their celebrations upstairs to one of the many vacant rooms.

Unusually, he hadn't felt the need to participate in the goings on. Dawn was still many hours away, but something compelled him to call it a night already. Frankly, he had even begun to feel a bit bored.

It was a regular Friday night in early December. The party had been fine, though Michael hadn't appreciated the gaudy decorations everyone seemed so fond of around this time of year. The people in attendance had been fine, too. Nothing particularly exciting, but he couldn't find fault with any of it either.

Still, something was off; he hadn't been able to feel comfortable. A growing feeling of unease filled his chest and he could not ignore it any longer. What exactly had sparked his restlessness, he wasn't sure.

Michael said his goodbyes, nodding at the odd acquaintance among the crowd of strangers, then made his way toward the exit.

"Aw, won't you stay a little longer?" A leggy blonde, who he had chatted to a little earlier, intercepted Michael on his way out. Her eyes were big, almost pleading as she spoke, her movements slightly uncoordinated.

Ordinarily, he might have considered her request, even if she was a bit too intoxicated for his liking. He liked his intimate partners to be alert, otherwise there was no joy in it for him. Still, she was beautiful, well dressed. Exactly his usual type.

But tonight, he just wasn't interested.

"I really must be off. I have some work—"

"You work Saturdays?" The woman cocked her head to the side and started twirling a lock of her hair around her index finger.

Michael paused. He wasn't used to being questioned on the validity of his excuses. Luckily, vampires had ways of dealing with that sort of thing.

"I'm afraid so," he spoke, while staring into the woman's eyes. The change came over him easily. He was still young in vampire terms, but his mental abilities were well developed.

The woman's demeanor changed almost instantly. The uncertainty in her eyes vanished. She became still and was now completely captivated until he released her from his influence.

"Okay." She sounded monotone, like she wasn't aware that she had responded out loud.

"Why don't you stay a little longer? The night is still young. Enjoy yourself," Michael suggested.

The woman blinked once, then continued to stare into his eyes.

"Go on," he urged. That was when he broke eye contact, consciously severing their connection.

She blinked again, then turned around and headed straight for the bar counter without turning back even once. Michael made his escape before anyone else could stop him.

He buttoned up his woolen overcoat as he stepped outside. It was a starless night; the dense cloud cover had made sure of that. There was a certain electricity in the air, which to him suggested it might be about to start snowing.

Michael took a deep breath and closed his eyes. Yes, something was definitely coming. Could that be what had made him feel off for most of the night?

The frosty air surrounding the bar he'd just left seemed heavy with a great many aromas. Things that humans might never notice; for example, the scent of what remained of the fallen autumn leaves from that one tree down the street.

Michael turned to face the opposite direction. Chinatown was at least a mile away, but he could smell the restaurants from here.

He was tempted to stretch his legs a little and sprint home as fast as only a vampire could, but the roads were still too busy. He couldn't risk someone watching him as he seemingly disappeared into thin air. The Council didn't take kindly to vampires exposing themselves to humans at the best of times. Ever since the big showdown between Michael's friend and mentor Alexander and Council leader Julius, they'd been under extra scrutiny. Julius would jump at the chance to punish Michael for supporting Alexander.

Things had really changed a lot in a short period of time, and not entirely for the better.

Michael opened his eyes again, resigned to the fact that he would either have to hail a cab or walk home at an excruciatingly slow, much more human-like pace.

He started to walk roughly in the direction of Hyde Park. If he found a quiet spot, he might still indulge himself in a little fun. As he crossed the busy street ahead, his nose caught a whiff of something unexpected, something metallic.

Blood.

His instincts took over. He turned on his heel and sped up a little as he followed the smell. A low whimper urged him to speed up even further, but he couldn't risk going any faster if he didn't want to make a spectacle of himself.

There was a dark passageway in between two large office buildings. He made his way through and found himself in a quiet courtyard, which housed a number of large garbage bins. A woman's foot peeked out from in between them. No human would have been able to see it in the dark, but Michael could.

Her breaths were labored and becoming shallower, and

her heartbeat was slowing. Michael pushed one of the bins aside and kneeled beside the woman, who lay face-down on the ground.

It was obvious to him now; she was barely clinging on to life. He carefully turned her onto her back. Her lips had a purple tinge and her skin looked dry and unusually pale for a human.

The two dark marks on her neck spoke volumes.

She'd been drained.

For but a split second, her eyelids fluttered open. She seemed to see him and opened her mouth to speak, but no sound came. Then she slipped back into unconsciousness.

Michael tensed up. He ought to leave, pretend he never found her. The last thing he needed was for someone to find him here, standing over a dying woman who had clearly been attacked by one of his own. But he couldn't bring himself to leave.

How pretty she was, how fragile, as she clung to her last shred of humanity.

Why had she ended up like this? Killing was against the rules. And discarding a drained body out in public where it could so easily be discovered? That was sacrilege.

His mind raced. Too many questions, not enough answers.

Michael gazed down at her face; the slightly parted lips, despite their unnatural color, still looked full and luxurious. As did the rest of her, actually. She made a beautiful corpse. Such a waste. This woman would have been a sight to behold before someone had decided to take her life for themselves.

He ran the back of his index finger along the side of her face. She twitched slightly, seemingly in reaction to his touch, causing him to pull away again.

No, he would not leave her, discarded among these bins of office refuse. This wasn't the end she deserved.

Michael closed his eyes and tried to focus. Her heartbeat had become irregular, as though her body was giving up the fight. If he didn't hurry, there wouldn't be any life left to save.

Before he fully realized what he was doing, Michael nicked a vein in his wrist and pressed the newly created wound against her lips.

"Drink," he whispered.

She was too far out of it, so he couldn't compel her to listen, but that wouldn't stop him.

Then, he picked up one of her arms and brought it to his own lips. He waited for what felt like forever. Was she too far gone already?

"Drink or you'll die!" he urged again, fully aware she likely couldn't even hear him.

Still, as more and more of his blood trickled out of the gash in his wrist, there was a subtle change in her. Her heartbeat seemed to strengthen. Her breaths became more controlled.

And then, out of nowhere, her free hand jerked up to grab his wrist and press it tightly against her mouth.

Finally, she drank in deep gulps as her body tried to recover what it had lost.

That was his cue.

He bit into the wrist he'd been holding already and allowed himself the smallest of tastes. That completed the cycle. The Ritual was done.

She became still again and let go of his arm, her hand flopping down onto her stomach. Her eyes had remained shut throughout; she probably hadn't even realized what had just happened.

He'd barely realized it too; he'd been acting purely on instinct. Now, as he stood up and inspected the smeared blood on his wrist, it hit him. He'd performed the Ritual. He'd created another vampire—tried to, anyway.

That was something he'd vowed he'd never take as lightly as his own maker had.

She wasn't out of the woods yet; in fact, he wouldn't know if she'd even survive the change until the following night, but for some strange reason, he'd jumped in and impulsively made the biggest decision of his immortal life so far.

Things would never be the same again.

———•———

Michael sank into one of the leather armchairs in the library and rested his head in his hands.

Neither Alexander, Michael's friend and mentor, nor his human consort, Cat, had said a word when he reached home carrying an unconscious half-turned human in his arms. Their expressions had spoken volumes. Now that she was safely tucked away in one of the bedrooms upstairs, Michael braced himself for the lecture he was about to hear.

"You brought a fledgling into this house. This house which you share with a human! Do you have any idea what you've done?" Alexander leaned forward and balled his fists. Cat walked up behind Alexander's chair and rested her hand on his shoulder.

"I couldn't very well leave her there to die in the street!" Michael was sorry for the situation he'd put everyone in, but what else could he have done?

Alexander shook his head. "You realize she's going to wake up thirsty. And Catherine…" He reached up and placed his hand on top of Cat's. "She's a Blood Bride. You know what that means. Her presence can be too much to resist for a grown vampire. A newborn won't be able to help themselves!"

Alexander was right, of course. It had taken a good while for Michael to learn to control his urges after Cat had first moved into the house. And he had been turned decades ago.

"Michael has a point too, you know," Cat spoke softly.

Michael looked up in surprise. He hadn't expected Cat to take his side. After all, she was the one who had the most to lose if things escalated.

"You're new to this. You've never been around a newly

made vampire before. They can't control themselves at the best of times!" Alexander argued.

"As you said, I'm a Blood Bride. Even ancient vampires seem to have a hard time controlling themselves once they catch a whiff of me." Cat shrugged and winked at Michael.

"It's dangerous. He's brought danger into our house!" Alexander gestured in Michael's direction.

"He couldn't just leave her to die, though."

The couple shared a look.

Michael shook his head as he thought back to the scene in the alley. How he had first discovered the woman.

"What was I supposed to do?" Michael asked.

Alexander's eyes were on him again. He pressed his lips together, clearly still displeased with Michael's actions, but he didn't respond. Perhaps he didn't have any answers either.

"You'll have to teach her everything I taught you," Alexander said finally.

Michael nodded. "I know."

"Catherine's safety depends on it."

Cat smiled subtly at Michael. At least she was on his side.

Michael had been skeptical when Alexander had first taken Cat as his consort. Especially since the leader of the Vampire Council himself, Julius, had wanted her for himself. Michael hadn't understood Alexander's reasoning for taking a risk so big. Of course, he'd sided with Alexander anyway; loyalty was important to him and he owed Alexander his life.

Now, when it was time for Alexander to support Michael's choice, it seemed that Cat's influence was the one thing tipping things in his favor. How ironic.

"I will make sure she doesn't harm anyone, especially Cat."

Cat nodded at Michael as she squeezed Alexander's shoulder. "It'll be fine. You worry too much," she said.

"I hope so."

"I promise I'll not let anything happen to her," Michael said. Although his promise was aimed at Cat, it was equally true for the mystery woman that lay in one of the bedrooms upstairs. He'd brought her here—helpless, like a wounded animal. He was responsible.

Alexander's words had affected him deeply. Should he have left her behind? No, that would have been utterly wrong. For the woman, as well as for the safety of their own kind. What if she'd been discovered there? What if human authorities had figured out who—or what—had killed her?

Michael didn't have a choice, and if necessary, he could justify himself to anyone. But that didn't mean that this would be easy. He tensed up at the prospect of what was to come.

Michael's own initiation into immortality had been difficult, at least until Alexander had taken him under his wing. He owed it to his woman to make her turning as easy as possible. But there was no way of predicting how she'd take it.

This little argument among friends was nothing in comparison to what might yet occur.

CHAPTER TWO

———— ◆ ————

She was sore when she woke up. Her muscles seemed tight to the point of being cramped, as though she had gone to the gym the day before. Not that she recalled ever going to a gym. Her thoughts were fuzzy, like she'd woken up in the middle of an intense dream, the details of which eluded her.

She opened her eyes and blinked a few times while waiting for her eyes to adjust. The room was dark, but she could still see her surroundings clearly.

The four-poster bed didn't look familiar, and neither did the decorative rosette in the center of the ceiling.

Where am I?

She winced as she lifted her upper body and rested on her elbows. Every inch of her felt like she was covered in bruises. Worst of all was her head. The shooting pain behind her eyes caused her vision to blur slightly with each heartbeat. Still, she was overwhelmed by all that she saw.

Beautiful period furniture, luxurious paintings, heavy embroidered drapes. Despite the lack of direct light, she could see the carved frame of the painting across the room in exquisite detail. She wasn't wearing glasses, was she? Surely, she should have felt the weight of them on the bridge of her nose. There was nothing there, though she felt compelled to confirm the same by touch.

She was certain that this wasn't her room.

She gently lowered herself down against the fluffy pillows again and closed her eyes. What did *her* room actually look like? Those details were much fuzzier than the sharp reality that surrounded her.

If this isn't my room, then how did I get here?

She heard a couple of muffled voices, perhaps originating from next door. Two men, having what sounded like an agitated conversation, though she could not make out the exact words. She didn't recognize either of their voices.

The more she thought about it, the more uneasy she grew. How had she ended up here?

Her heart started to beat faster, so fast that she should have been out of breath and perhaps faint. Instead, she somehow felt... stronger. Could that even be?

Everything still hurt, of course, like she'd been hit by a bus. Could she have been in an accident before someone brought her here?

She pressed her lips together and fought through the intense pain as she lifted herself again and slipped out of bed. As she set herself down onto the lacquered wooden floor, it was like an electric jolt passed through the soles of her feet and all the way up through her legs and torso. It wasn't cold as such, nor was it unpleasant, but it was somehow different than any floor she'd ever walked barefoot on.

The voices next door had calmed down a bit, like their

debate had turned into a more restrained, controlled conversation. As she listened for more, she could hear the other sounds that filled the strange house she was in. Ticking, of a clock perhaps. Rustling leaves. Creaks and scratches which she could not place nor identify.

And the scents that surrounded her were different from anything she'd ever experienced too. She could pick up everything, from the lacquer of the floor, to the fabric softener used on the sheets and the rubber soles on the pair of shoes in the corner. She could even smell the plaster and wallpaper on the walls, which was strange. She'd never paid attention to the scent of wallpaper before.

She shook her head. What a strange place this was, where everything smelled somehow more intense than normal. What did her own home smell like? She couldn't recall. She felt like Alice in Wonderland, exploring a place where the strange was normal, and she seemed to be the odd one out.

Who am I?

She wandered across the room to an elegant rosewood dresser and looked at herself in the mirror. Her reflection was the first thing that looked somewhat familiar in here.

Who am I?

She leaned forward and studied her features. Smooth skin, silky hair—this wasn't how she usually woke up, was it? No sign of puffiness around the eyes, not a single tangle in her shoulder-length locks. And what was she wearing? A long cotton nightgown, rather old fashioned. That couldn't be hers, could it?

It was like she had been groomed to perfection before being put to rest in here. Creepy.

Anna, nice to meet you! She herself had said those words not too long ago, smiled, and stretched out her hand at someone. But at whom? Whom had she introduced herself to?

Anna rubbed her eyes and then studied herself again. No, that was all she had. The only memory she could conjure was of her first name.

If she couldn't remember who she was or where she was from, the least she ought to do was find out where she was now. Anna took a deep breath and straightened her back. Surely and steadily, her muscles seemed to relax a bit. Every step loosened her up a bit more.

Anna approached the door and paused to listen for those voices again before turning the handle. It seemed safe enough. The two men seemed occupied with each other. She would be careful, and they probably wouldn't even hear her.

As she pressed her hand down, she flinched at the horrible creak of the handle. Then, to her relief, she found that the door was unlocked; she was able to push it open and create even more of a racket. These people, whoever they were, should really do something about their noisy doors!

As soon as she pushed it open a bit more, she found herself blinded by the bright chandelier hanging in the center of the hallway ahead. *What the hell? Who puts bulbs this bright into a chandelier?*

She squinted as her eyes adjusted. It took a few painful moments before she could focus properly on what lay ahead.

The hallway was more of the same luxury she'd found in the bedroom. Paintings and expensive looking wallpaper adorned the walls, and there was a cornice edging the ceiling and a rosette just above the chandelier. Whoever lived here had made the place look less like a house and more like a palace. Anna couldn't decide if it was tasteful or kitsch.

She carefully moved forward, tiptoeing so that she wouldn't tip off the men she'd heard talking earlier. Come to think of it, they had now stopped talking. Had they heard her?

She rested her hand against the wall and listened. The opening of a bottle, followed by the rush of liquid as it poured out. The sound was unmistakable; she'd heard it so many times before in her line of work.

That was it. She had worked as a waitress. Anna clearly saw a glimpse of her own hands, opening bottles and pouring glasses of champagne. She opened her eyes and still found herself alone in an empty hallway, though. Like she'd just imagined that sound.

She rubbed her temples, attempting to dull the ache. Clearly, whatever had happened to her had made her lose her mind. Hallucinations, fragmented memories. Would it all come back to her soon, like it did in the movies?

Those same men started talking again and Anna breathed a sigh of relief. As long as they carried on chatting, they would hopefully be oblivious to whatever she was up to. No way was she going to let herself get caught sneaking around a strange house without first figuring out where she was and what she was up against. She had to make sure she was safe first, before confronting any of these people.

Who knew, perhaps they were the ones responsible for her fragile condition in the first place! Perhaps they'd attacked her before bringing her here?

Anna bit her lip and a rush of warm liquid burst through her skin and into her mouth. Blood.

Strangely, the wound she had just created was the only spot on her body that didn't currently hurt. She tiptoed forward toward a mirror further up the hallway.

Her bottom lip was stained bright red. She leaned forward to get a better look. There wasn't any sign of a cut or split. She licked the blood away and found that her lips were full and flawless, much more so than normal. Then she opened her mouth and inspected her teeth. White, straight, perfect.

But the canines…

She held her breath and touched her teeth with the tip of her finger. Razor sharp and longer than what seemed possible. Was this some kind of joke?

Had these freaks kidnapped her and done some kind of

cosmetic dentistry on her? She shook her head. This must be yet another thing she was only imagining. Her mind was playing tricks on her, but she wouldn't let it get her down. She had to stay focused on the one thing that was important: figuring where she was and why she was here. And perhaps she could even find a way out.

The voices grew louder the further she tiptoed up the hallway. Finally, she found herself at the top of an impressive wooden staircase leading to the lower level of the house. They were down there somewhere. Just as Anna was about to take the first step down, a whiff of something irresistible caught her attention. Perfume? Food?

She turned around and scanned the other hallway, leading in the opposite direction of the landing. That was where it had come from. Anna took a deep breath and closed her eyes. Better than the bakery she'd walk past on her way home from work. *Cobbled streets, dark facades, except for a modern looking building with large windows that would produce the most amazing scents. Vanilla, chocolate, cinnamon…*

Anna opened her eyes again. Another clue. Whatever her life looked like, she lived somewhere near a bakery. Perhaps all of her memories would come back soon enough.

She wasn't sure how long she'd been reminiscing for. The scent had dissipated, leaving her once again alone atop the stairs. Down below, she heard the distinct click and deafening creak of a door. As nice as everything looked, simple maintenance clearly wasn't a priority in this house.

Footsteps echoed against the walls downstairs. Anna hid behind the balustrade and covered her ears to drown out the noise. It might have been smarter to retreat back to her room, but she simply had to catch a glimpse of whoever's house this was. She squinted to see through the bright light overhead. That was when she saw him.

A dark-haired man in an elegant black suit cut straight across the hall downstairs.

"You take care of it, you hear me, Michael?" he said.

"Of course, Alexander," another man responded, just out of view.

Anna pressed her lips together. Was that about her? Was this Michael fellow meant to take care of *her*?

The man left, and the double doors shut behind him with an almighty racket. Anna breathed a sigh of relief once it was over. Her poor ears. Were all of these people hard of hearing? Did they not notice how incredibly loud everything was in here?

She got up and rubbed her back. Still a bit sore, but her body felt a lot better than it had when she'd just woken up.

Anna was about to take the first step down to explore more of the house, perhaps even make a run for the door, when a figure appeared in the corner of her eye down at the end of the staircase.

"I'd been wondering when you'd wake up," the man said.

Anna flinched, only to find that she'd backed into a wall and couldn't go further. Within the blink of an eye, he had joined her on the upstairs landing.

Two pale blue eyes looked down at her briefly before glancing in the direction of the hallway she'd just come from.

He was tall and flawlessly handsome. His pale skin seemed to glisten slightly in the bright light that surrounded the two of them. If she hadn't just woken up with a wiped mind and a full-on body ache in a strange house, she might have found him attractive. Maybe.

There was something familiar about him, but she could not place him.

"Who are you? Where am I? Why am I here?" Anna asked.

The man's eyes darted back and forth between the hallway and her face. "How about we talk somewhere more comfortable. I'm Michael Odell, by the way. What's your name?"

Anna took a deep breath and studied his face. He couldn't even look her in the eye while he spoke. He was hiding something. Maybe he'd let his guard down if she played along just a little bit.

"Okay, Michael. I'm Anna." Her hand itched to shake his, just to see what he'd feel like in this strange heightened state she was experiencing, but she resisted the urge.

This wasn't the time to give in to temptation. First, she needed an explanation.

CHAPTER THREE

Michael could tell Anna had only grudgingly agreed to head back into her newly appointed bedroom with him. As they walked down the hall, he'd tried to explain everything he knew about the attack and what had followed, failing miserably.

"I'm not sure I understand," Anna said. "What exactly happened?"

Michael could hardly stand looking at her. Something about this woman—Anna, no last name, as she'd introduced herself—threw him off balance. He'd lost not just his *game*, but his entire sense of self around her. It was infuriating.

She was beautiful, but that was hardly a valid reason to lose himself in her presence.

"As I said, when I found you, you were in a bad way. There was really nothing I could do, other than perform the Ritual," he stammered.

Gone was the confident vampire who could walk into any bar, any party, any social function at all, and not just fit in effortlessly, but steer any interaction in his favor. Conversation, flattery, and seduction had not just been words in his vocabulary, they were all part of the same art Michael had sought to master over the years. Beautiful women were his *thing*, along with gourmet meals and fine wines. In his human life, he'd never succeeded at obtaining the high flying lifestyle he so craved, though not for lack of trying. It wasn't until Alexander had taken him in that he had found everything he'd been searching for. In immortality, he seemed to have the world at his feet.

But right now with Anna, none of it mattered. It was like his slate had been wiped clean. He couldn't even hypnotize her to save face. He felt completely and utterly inept.

"What are you telling me?" Anna demanded and stared at him with arms folded. "I don't remember any of this."

"I…" Michael tried to focus, but his mind didn't cooperate. Instead of feeding him the necessary words to make her understand what had happened while she was unconscious, all he could think of was old memories.

Don't fly too close to the sun, you might get burned—these words rang in his ears, decades after he'd last heard his father say them. His parents had been the more practical, down-to-earth sort, who never understood his more materialistic ambitions. And although the context was quite different now, these words had never seemed more relevant to Michael than right at this moment.

Michael looked into her amber eyes, briefly, before looking away again.

"You basically died. Now you're reborn."

"I don't understand. What have you done to me?" She'd tensed up as she glared at him. Michael couldn't tell if her reaction was the result of fear or anger.

He shook his head; he wasn't explaining it quite right. "You're immortal. You're a vampire now."

"Vampires don't exist," Anna argued. "You must think I'm stupid."

Michael's frustration peaked. "Wanna bet? Anyway, you don't have to take my word for it. Go on, look at the facts."

Anna started pacing around the room. "Facts! How ridiculous. I wake up here alone with no memory of how I got here or where I'm from, hearing voices through the walls, with weird pointy things stuck to my teeth and you're trying to tell me… I don't believe it!"

She stopped in front of the mirror. "It's all a trick, it has to be. See! I can see my reflection, right there."

Michael sighed. This was never easy. But at least most people were somewhat lucid when they underwent the Ritual. They remembered, even if they didn't understand what they'd gone through.

Anna didn't even seem to remember who she had been in her human life.

"It's a lot to take in. I understand. You'll feel better once you feed," Michael said. He was trying his best to stay calm, he really was. By God, as attractive as she was, this woman really knew how to push his buttons.

"Feed? Don't tell me you expect me to drink blood next! Look, mister. I don't know who you think you are, but I'm not participating in this perverted little game of yours. I want to go home, right now!"

You're going to get burned, the little voice in Michael's head insisted. He shook his head, trying to silence it.

"By all means then, I'll take you home right now. Remind me, where exactly *is* home?" Michael snapped. He regretted his outburst as soon as he saw Anna's face.

She retreated and sat down on the bed and rested her head in her hands. Clearly, she had no idea how to answer his question.

"Look, I'm sorry. That wasn't fair," Michael said.

He approached her and hesitated a moment before touching her shoulder. He wanted to help her so badly, but at the same time, he was frustrated beyond belief.

She flinched and shook him off.

"I just don't get it. Is everyone insane around here?" Anna said.

Michael sighed and sat down next to her, making sure he kept a safe distance. "You could say that," he mumbled, more to himself than her.

Her hand trembled as she reached for her fangs, touching first one, then the other. She let out a soft *ouch* when she nicked her finger tip, causing it to bleed.

"I know it doesn't seem like it, but I did what I thought was best. You had been attacked. I found you when you were moments away from death, and I didn't know what else to do," Michael spoke softly. He was trying to convince himself of his words, as much as her.

"Assuming I believe you—which I *don't*—please explain everything again. I'm immortal? What does that even mean?" Anna turned to face him, then put her wounded finger against her lips and licked away the blood.

It was mesmerizing to watch.

Michael shook his head. He had to snap out of it. It was deeply inappropriate to think of her that way. "Uh, yeah. Of course. Well, it's much like the stories, except for the bit about having no reflection. You'll be awake at night, you need blood to survive, you won't age…"

Anna stopped and looked at her index finger, which was once again unmarked, as though she'd never wounded herself at all. Michael watched her from the corner of his eye.

"Sunlight, garlic, holy water, stakes through the heart, those are the only things that'll harm me?" Anna asked.

Michael let out a laugh, then quickly recovered. "Sorry. Well, sunlight will definitely kill you, garlic and holy water, not so much. A stake through the heart—that's very old school. I'm not sure what that'll do, maybe sting for a while?"

Anna frowned and turned to face him. "So I'll have to murder people to survive?" she asked. Her eyes were wide, giving her face a certain innocence. She had only looked this helpless back when she'd briefly regained consciousness back in that filthy alley.

Michael shook his head and tried to reach for her again, causing her to recoil.

She didn't trust him. Not that he could blame her.

"No, we don't kill. It's against the rules."

"So how do you drink blood then?" she asked.

"Well, as you get to grips with your new powers, you'll be able to hypnotize humans. They won't feel a thing."

She looked away from him and stared at the floor in front of the bed. "Okay…"

Michael relaxed a bit. Perhaps she was ready to accept the truth now.

"And the other guy I saw downstairs, he's a vampire too?" she asked.

"Yeah, Alexander. He found me when I was still a fledgling. Taught me everything I know."

She nodded and continued to stare at the floor in silence. Neither of them said a word for at least a minute.

Anna took a deep breath. "You lads are insane. There's no other explanation." She straightened her back and folded her arms again.

Michael opened his mouth to say something, but he had nothing. He rested his elbows on his thighs and shook his head. He'd done what he could. This woman was incredibly stubborn. She'd have to figure out the truth for herself.

He got up and walked toward the door.

"Wait, you're not leaving me, are you?" Anna called out behind him.

He gestured at her to wait. Realizing that actually he didn't need to follow the usual precautions that he took around humans, he broke into a sprint, straight to the kitchen downstairs. He grabbed a few cold cuts and a steak from the fridge, depositing the whole lot on a plate. Whether she liked it or not, Anna needed to feed. Hopefully she'd realize this as soon as she saw the meat.

He was back in her bedroom within the blink of an eye. He'd hoped that this little display of his superhuman speed would convince her, but when he looked at her, still sitting in place on the bed, he didn't see recognition in her eyes. Whatever he'd just tried to demonstrate, she hadn't noticed anything strange about it.

Michael wished he could ask Alexander for advice, but that wasn't an option. He'd taken Cat away for the week, in an attempt to keep her safe, and he was still angry with him to boot. Michael was on his own. They'd all ended up in an impossible situation together, thanks to his impulsive decision to turn this woman.

All he could hope for now was that Anna would see the truth and come around to accepting her new situation before Alexander returned. Otherwise… Well, otherwise Michael wasn't quite sure what would happen. He'd have to fix this situation he'd created. If Cat wasn't safe in the same house as Anna, he'd have to relocate her somehow.

And the entire conversation he'd just tried to have with Anna suggested was that she wasn't easily convinced of anything. How would he convince her to leave with him without creating a scene? What a headache.

Michael held the plate in her direction. "You must be hungry. Please, help yourself."

Anna eyed him suspiciously, then glanced down at the

food. Her eyes rested on the raw steak.

Michael remembered clearly what it had been like when he was freshly turned. Every sense was almost painfully heightened. She wouldn't be able to resist the juicy meat, not for long anyway.

"It's raw," she said.

"You're very observant," he said, then immediately regretted his tone.

She glared at him, then looked back down at the plate.

"It'll do you good. If you don't believe me, that's fine. Try it and you'll find out for yourself," he added, doing his best to sound patient. It was difficult, nigh impossible. He wanted nothing more than to force her to eat it already. Why couldn't she just take his word for it?

After a few more seconds of indecision, Anna finally seemed to give in. She took the plate from him and sniffed the meat, closing her eyes as the scent of blood no doubt overwhelmed her senses. When she opened her eyes again, they had turned a deep shade of red.

Blood lust. Finally.

That was how Michael had reacted too, when he had awoken a newly created vampire and stood face to face with his first meal. Only, there had been no one to guide him, no one to provide him with a safe meal option. He'd acted purely on instinct and almost killed the man he'd tried to drink from. It had been a disaster.

"Eat. Trust me," he urged.

Anna didn't hesitate any longer. She scarfed down

everything on the plate, even licking off the juices that ended up on her fingers.

"Weird. I've never been much of a meat eater," she mumbled.

Michael took the plate from her and observed her as she pulled her legs up onto the bed and curled up against the pillows.

"So… sleepy…" she whispered.

Michael continued to watch her for a moment. That was what had happened to him too. It was quite a shock to the system, digesting your first meal after the change. Perhaps things between them would improve once she had more of a chance to rest.

She was quite something, even if she was his fledgling and he was her maker. Feisty, too. If only the circumstances of their meeting had been different…

"I'll be downstairs if you need me," he said.

"Mhmm."

Michael didn't look back as he left the room, pulling the door shut behind him. Out of habit, he checked the large grandfather clock on the landing. It was just before nine o'clock. Ordinarily, he'd be getting ready to go out by now. Not tonight, though.

His nights of carefree and unapologetic hedonism were over.

Michael had never been particularly responsible, but going forward, he wouldn't have a choice. And that realization worried him, possibly even more so than the prospect of having Anna argue with him some more upon waking up.

CHAPTER FOUR

Once again, Anna woke up to the sound of muffled voices. But it wasn't two men this time; instead, it was a woman and a man. And she could hear them more clearly, so much so that she could follow the whole conversation word-for-word.

"What do you want?" the male voice, which Anna recognized as Michael's, asked.

"Council business. Where is my dear brother?" the female demanded.

"Out. He took Catherine with him. I'm afraid you'll have to put up with me instead."

Anna held her breath as she continued to listen. It was obvious from his tone that whoever this woman was, Michael not only knew her, but knew her well enough to dislike her.

"Very well. It has come to our attention that some—shall we say—*outsiders* have arrived in the city. If they're even aware of our customs and laws, they are blatantly ignoring them. *Humans* have been affected."

That last bit made Anna's ears perk up even more. She was no longer content waiting around in this bedroom, she had to see this visitor for herself. The way she had emphasized the word 'humans' was very strange indeed. Could it be that this visitor also believed in the nonsense story Michael had tried to tell her earlier, about the lot of them being vampires?

"You don't say," Michael responded. His sarcasm wasn't lost on Anna, and she couldn't even see the two of them yet. She hurried out of bed and sneaked out the door as fast as she could. Thankfully, Anna's body ache had mostly subsided as she'd slept, allowing her more stealth and speed than before.

"In fact, would it be safe to say one such human is here right now?" the woman spoke up again.

Suddenly self-conscious, Anna paused just before reaching the top of the stairs. No, she had come this far, she would take a look at this new stranger for herself. It was bad enough that Michael and the other man were deluded about who or what they were, but now this woman seemed equally out of touch with reality.

"Is dear old Gillian still surveilling us then?" Michael asked. "Either way, there are no humans here."

Anna kneeled down and peeked through the balustrade, only to find Michael already staring at her. His expression didn't change one bit; the man had the perfect poker face. A perfectly handsome, infuriating poker face.

Seeing how he had already anticipated her curiosity annoyed her. How arrogant he was.

"The Council has eyes and ears everywhere, as you well know," the slender, dark-haired woman said. She stood with her back toward Anna, her shoulders pulled back, suggesting amazing posture. Anna was almost disappointed she couldn't catch a glimpse of the woman's face.

"Well, Lucille, I don't know what to tell you. If there were a human in here, I'm sure you would have smelled her… or him." Michael maintained eye contact with Anna as he spoke, making her feel uneasy.

Look away, or you'll tip this Lucille woman off! Anna frowned to make her point.

Finally, Michael did stop staring at her.

Anna breathed a sigh of relief. She wasn't sure why he was affecting her. These people were clearly nuts. If only she could get out of here and head home. Inconveniently, she still didn't remember where *home* was exactly, or she might have been able to make a run for it.

"Very well, have it your way. You'll know where to find the Council if you come across any of these unwanted visitors, as well as their victims. I don't have to remind you that Julius expects your loyalty now more than ever. And that goes for my brother as well."

Michael nodded. His expression had softened slightly, making him look just a little less arrogant than before. Still, Anna wasn't sure what to think. These people were weird, untrustworthy.

Lucille nodded and pushed the two double doors open wide as she left. They had barely swung back into position when Michael stood up on the landing in front of Anna.

"Oh!" She took a step back and tried to regain her composure. How had he moved so quickly? "Who was that?"

"Lucille Amboise. Julius turned her around the same time as Alexander, so they consider themselves siblings."

Anna wanted to argue. *Turned her.* Ridiculous. Michael was really intent on dragging this fantasy out as long as he could manage. "And what is this Council she kept referring to? What do they want with me?"

"The Vampire Council, led by Julius. Well, they make sure that we follow the rules. Like I said before, we're not supposed to—"

"Yeah, not supposed to kill, right?"

"Right." Michael smiled and looked right at her for a moment. As soon as he did, something weird happened inside her chest. Was it nerves? Excitement? No way was she going to allow herself to develop a soft spot for a lunatic!

"It appears that the Council is on the trail of the vampires who did this to you. They take that sort of thing very seriously."

"So not only have you turned me into a *vampire* to *save me*, it was *vampires* who put me in the position to need saving in the first place? Funny how there are all of a sudden a lot of vampires running around London." Anna folded her arms and cocked her head to the side. She didn't have much patience left. Not for him, or his nonsense.

Michael shrugged. "Don't believe me, it hardly matters at this point. Answer me one thing, though: that bloody steak did make you feel better, didn't it?"

Anna pressed her lips together tightly. She wanted to prove him wrong so desperately, but the worst part was that he was right. She did feel better now, and the steak hadn't been as disgusting as she'd thought either. Both those realizations annoyed her to no end.

"Perhaps I just needed more rest," she said at last.

"More rest. Sure." Michael shook his head slowly, then raised both his hands up in the air. "Look, between you refusing to believe a word I'm saying and Lucille turning up and interrogating me, this is turning into quite the trying evening. Perhaps it's best we talk about something else."

What else was there to talk about, though? She'd woken up feeling better, but there was still so much she didn't understand about her current situation. And she didn't even remember the necessary details to allow her to leave yet. She was stuck here, with him, until she could formulate a plan.

"I'm going downstairs to the library for a drink. You may join me if you like." Just like that, Michael had cut their conversation short.

"Wearing a nightgown?" Anna called after him, as he made his way down the stairs at a breakneck speed.

"Check the wardrobe in your room. There might be something in there," he said as he continued sprinting downstairs and to the left, just out of Anna's sight. God, how he annoyed her.

Within moments, she had returned to the bedroom—the one place in this house that was starting to look somewhat familiar—and found something passable to wear. As she undressed, she couldn't help but check herself out in the mirror. She'd changed. It didn't seem possible, but somehow, her body had smoothed out somewhat. Curves that had been there for as long as she could remember had firmed up. Imperfections had been wiped away.

She barely recognized her reflection, something which she might have explained away with the memory loss that she'd woken up with. Only, she clearly remembered what she used to look like. In excruciating, painful detail.

And it was those details, those little things she had found fault with before, which were missing now.

Gone was the cellulite, the odd marks and scars, even the stretch marks. Caps could explain the pointy teeth, perhaps a chemical peel had been responsible for her glowing complexion. And her hair? That could have been brushed and styled while she'd been unconscious.

But there was nothing in the world that could change her body to this extent, was there? There was no cure for stretch marks or cellulite. These two things plagued even skinnier girls. Anna was a lot of things, but even in her changed form, she still wasn't skinny.

Could it be that perhaps Michael's explanation wasn't so far-fetched after all? Could she actually have been changed into something supernatural...? Super-*human*?

It still seemed impossible, and yet it would explain a lot. Her sensitive hearing—she'd been able to overhear entire conversations taking place halfway across this massive house. Her changed physical form—pointy teeth and impossibly perfect skin. And her appetite for raw meat.

Anna shook her head and pulled on a pair of pants and a pullover she'd found in the wardrobe. These didn't look or feel like they were hers, but they would serve their purpose and make her feel just a little bit less vulnerable. It was awkward having to talk to a stranger wearing nothing more than a nightgown, even if it was nearly floor length and quite modest.

She took a deep breath and glanced at her reflection one last time before heading downstairs. She hoped that whatever drink Michael had been referring to would be something familiar, and not, God forbid, some unfortunate soul's blood.

On the way down, she caught a glimpse of the grand standing clock which towered over the landing. It was almost four o'clock. But inside the house, with its heavy drapes and brightly lit interior, Anna had no sense of time at all. If she hadn't noticed the thick cover of darkness outside as Lucille left, she wouldn't have known if it was four in the afternoon or in the morning.

She had obviously never been downstairs and had no idea of the layout, but her feet carried her automatically through the grand reception room with its elegant period settees and armchairs toward a heavy carved door that led to the library. Inside, Michael awaited.

He looked up the second she'd pushed the door open.

"There you are," he said.

Without warning, he picked up an empty glass from the table beside his leather armchair and flung it in Anna's direction. She was about to duck out of the way and let loose on him, when she realized that she had caught the glass, effortlessly, in her left hand.

"You threw a glass at my head!" she complained. "What the hell were you thinking?"

Michael's lips fluttered almost imperceptibly, as though he was suppressing a smile. "You caught it. Still unconvinced of your changed state?" he asked.

Anna wanted to bite her bottom lip, but then remembered the sharp teeth and resulting bleeding from earlier and stopped herself. How smug he was. Unfortunately, he had a point.

"Fine." She'd barely said the word, and a bottle zipped through the air in her direction. She still wasn't prepared, but at least it hadn't startled her as much as the glass. She caught it by the neck in her other hand.

"Pour yourself a drink. We have a lot to talk about." Michael said.

Anna scrutinized the label. It looked old, expensive. She walked across to the empty chair next to Michael and put the glass down. Then she opened the cap of the bottle and became overwhelmed as the aromas hit her. Woody, earthy, hints of sweetness and spice. It was brandy, that was certain, but she'd never smelled a vintage quite like it.

"Whoa," she mumbled, then glanced sideways at Michael, who was observing her, half full glass in hand.

"Your senses are much stronger now," he remarked.

She poured some of the amber liquid into the glass, which she now recognized as an expensive antique as well. To think that he'd just thrown it across the room like it was nothing. Rich people! What if she'd dropped it?

"How is this even possible," she whispered as she brought the glass to her lips.

The moment the brandy hit her tongue, she knew that somehow it was. Everything she'd rejected before had to be true. She wasn't quite sure how and why she'd ended up here, beyond what Michael had tried to tell her. She didn't even know exactly what her life had looked like earlier— she just knew that things would never be the same.

CHAPTER FIVE

Thank God.

Michael closed his eyes and took a sip from his glass. He hadn't been completely sure that it would work, but his reckless little stunt seemed to have convinced her. At the very least, it had planted the seed of doubt in her mind and caused her to stop arguing.

They sat in silence as Anna savored every last drop of the brandy. It was Alexander's stash, but he wouldn't mind. Not if it helped in getting Anna ready to deal with her new condition and most importantly, control her urges around Catherine once the two of them returned home.

And although vampires weren't affected by alcohol like humans were, sitting together and sharing a drink had a certain therapeutic value.

Michael had gone about it all wrong. Instead of taking a moment to understand that this woman had woken up confused in a strange house, surrounded by strangers, in a body that possibly felt as strange to her as everything else, he'd tried to force her into believing him.

Of course that hadn't worked.

His own transformation had been the exact opposite. Michael had woken up a vampire on his own, without a maker to guide him. Though he did remember what had happened during his last moments as a mortal, he had nobody to explain things. Everything, from the increased strength and speed to the boost to all his senses, he had discovered for himself.

That was why he wanted to spare Anna the confusion and pain of making mistakes. And in doing so, he'd cornered her and not given her the chance to process things. Now he knew that both approaches were equally wrong. He was ready to pull back. If it was space and freedom she needed, he was willing to give it to her.

What was the rush, anyway? They were immortal. Time didn't have the same meaning to their kind as it did to humans.

Anna leaned toward the side table and poured herself another drink.

"Refill?" she asked.

Michael lifted his glass to demonstrate that he still had some and continued to observe her. She had an elegance about her that he'd only just allowed himself to notice. The way she poured the drink—stopping at exactly the right level both times—suggested she'd performed the same action many times over. Perhaps this offered a clue to her human identity?

Anna wasn't his usual type; she wasn't easily impressed by anyone, least of all him. The clothes he'd found her in were simple, with not a designer label in sight. That told him that either she couldn't afford expensive clothes and accessories, or she didn't care for them.

Basically, she was his exact opposite. Michael himself

loved to surround himself with beautiful things. The luxury he lived in now compensated for the simple lifestyle he'd left behind upon being turned.

He clearly recalled the first time Alexander had brought him here, into his beautiful and unapologetically luxurious villa. Where he had reacted with instant awe and appreciation, Anna seemed to look at it all with a much more skeptical eye. Just the way she'd inspected the bottle and the old cut crystal snifter spoke volumes.

"Have you started remembering more?" Michael asked.

She shrugged. "I don't know. It's all very fuzzy."

Michael took her response as a sign she wasn't ready to discuss it.

So they continued to sit in silence for a while.

"There was a guy with red eyes," Anna said finally.

Michael straightened himself and leaned toward Anna, waiting for more.

She turned to face him, her eyes wide with fear. "I wasn't the only woman there."

"Where? What was the place like?" Michael asked.

Anna looked away at nothing in particular and blinked a few times.

"Don't know," she whispered. "It was dark."

Considering the state she was in when he found her, it was probably for the best if she never remembered everything that happened to her. Still, she was the only one who could offer clues regarding who these vampires were and where they were hiding out.

They were interrupted by the library door swinging open. Lucille had returned, this time unannounced and without invitation. *Bloody great.*

"I knew it," Lucille snapped as soon as she saw Anna. "I knew you weren't being totally truthful with me earlier!"

Michael rolled his eyes. "You asked if there was a mortal in the house. I only answered your question."

Anna gave him a concerned look. Lucille was unpleasant company, but she wouldn't do anything to harm a fellow vampire. They hadn't broken any rules; the strange vampires who had attacked Anna were the ones who should be worried.

Michael patted Anna's hand briefly in an attempt to reassure her, then immediately withdrew. A funny sensation had passed from her hand into his. It was unnervingly intense, but *so* tempting. He avoided eye contact with her and faced Lucille again in an attempt to divert his attention away from Anna. This wasn't the time to give his carnal desires free reign. She was his fledgling, for Pete's sake.

"Alexander should really ask for his spare keys back," Michael muttered under his breath.

Lucille scoffed. "As if I need keys to come in here."

Michael got up and offered her his seat. "Since we're all here now, why don't you make yourself comfortable? I'll get us another chair."

Lucille eyed Anna suspiciously. "What does she know?"

Michael grabbed the chair that stood in front of the

large desk at the back of the library and placed it near Anna. The entire maneuver was over within the blink of a human eye.

"Painfully little, I'm afraid. She's been suffering from a spot of memory loss since the attack."

"I'm right here, you know!" Anna protested. "I can speak for myself."

"I apologize," Michael mumbled, then gestured at her to continue.

"I was just telling Michael that I remember a man with glowing red eyes," Anna said.

Lucille glanced at Michael. "That's hardly groundbreaking. They were drinking her blood, after all."

Anna shrugged. "As you might imagine, I'm a bit new to this. Only trying to be helpful."

Michael sighed. "Red eyes are a sign of blood lust in vampires. Happens whenever we're thirsty," he explained.

"Ah." Anna shrugged. "Well that's all I remember for now. And that they had captured more women."

Lucille nodded. "Fine." She faced Michael again. "Now, if you don't mind sharing with me where you found her?"

"My name is Anna," Anna interjected.

Michael suppressed a little smile. It was obvious that Lucille's abrasiveness had rubbed Anna the wrong way. They had one more thing to agree on there.

If he had a choice, he wouldn't even be entertaining Lucille. Sadly, one had to humor the Council's Enforcer, especially when she arrived on Julius' orders. Plus,

Alexander owed her, meaning Michael did as well.

"Don't know the address, but I can show you the place," Michael said.

Lucille nodded. "Dawn is still a few hours away. No time like the present."

Michael shot Anna a reassuring look. "We won't be long."

"Wait just a minute! You're not thinking of leaving me here?"

"I don't think—" Lucille started to argue.

Anna got up, both hands raised in protest. "Unacceptable. I'm coming with you."

Michael shrugged. He'd had a good taste of how stubborn Anna could be when she'd first woken up. It was unlikely that he could talk her out of it.

"She's not ready!" Lucille complained.

"You're not hungry, are you?" Michael approached Anna, who now stood tall with her hands on her hips.

Anna shook her head. The way her hair fell around her face, she looked fierce. Determined. Sexy. Michael averted his gaze instantly. His thoughts were inappropriate. Plus, he couldn't allow let himself get distracted in Lucille's presence.

"See? No problem. She's already eaten today," Michael told Lucille.

Lucille's concerns were valid, since Anna had no idea of the temptation the outside world offered. But how much trouble could she really get into with two strong vampires accompanying her? If anything happened, they'd take care of it.

"Whatever." Lucille didn't sound convinced.

It didn't matter to Michael if she was. Just hours into her new life, Anna already was a force to be reckoned with. It pleased him greatly that Anna's rebellious nature was now aimed at Lucille and not at him anymore.

"Follow my lead," Michael whispered to Anna. "You'll be safe."

"Of course I'll be safe. I'm immortal now, aren't I?" Anna grinned.

Michael was about to interject that immortal didn't mean invincible, but decided to let it go. They'd have plenty of time to go through the finer points of being a vampire later.

Together, the three of them left, sprinting through the city faster than the human eye could see. Luckily, moving at superhuman speed was the one thing that came easy to newly turned vampires. Deliberately slowing things down to fit into human society? Not so much.

It didn't take them long to reach the courtyard where Michael had found Anna only hours earlier. At this time of night, the streets were empty enough that their activities went unseen.

The smell of blood still hung heavy in the air.

"Holy shit," Anna said, covering her mouth. Her eyes glowed red. "Is that me? My blood?"

"Told you she wasn't ready," Lucille said, folding her

arms.

Michael shot her a nasty glance. "Not much of it was left, but yes."

Anna wrinkled her nose and inhaled deeply. "How could you resist it? Oh my God, how did you not tear me to pieces and drink the last drops?"

Michael glanced over at Lucille, who had wandered off to start investigating.

"It takes a little while, but you'll learn to resist it too."

"Okay, but why would you want to?" Anna rambled. "I mean, it smells so… delicious. Why wouldn't you want to just give in?"

Anna breathed in deeply again and sharply turned her head away from him. Her body seemed to have tensed up as she stared in the direction of the main road, just a dozen or so feet away. Michael followed her line of sight. Footsteps approached. Human footsteps.

"This isn't the time," Michael said.

Anna snapped her head in his direction for just a split second, then turned away again. "So tempting. I can smell it."

Michael reached for Anna's arm. "Lucille. If you don't mind…"

Lucille joined him and held Anna back from the other side.

"Don't you say it," Michael warned her under his breath. He did *not* need another lecture right now.

For a tense thirty seconds or so, the three of them

stood in silence, Michael and Lucille holding Anna back, until the human had passed their position and his footsteps faded.

"Whoa. Okay." Anna's body relaxed underneath Michael's grip. "I'm okay."

Her eyes were once more the same warm amber color he had tried to avoid catching a glimpse of for most of the night. The threat was over.

"I'm sorry, I don't know what came over me," she muttered.

Lucille let go of her and silently went about her business again, inspecting bits of paper and other assorted rubbish strewn around the spot where Anna's body had been dumped.

"It's perfectly normal. You'll get used to it," Michael tried to reassure her.

"I could have. Oh God." Anna covered her face with her hands. "If you hadn't stopped me, who knows what I would have done."

I know exactly what you would have done. The same thing I did during my first night.

Michael didn't respond. Airing his own dirty laundry in front of Lucille wouldn't help anyone.

"You don't need us anymore, do you?" Michael called out to her.

Lucille shook her head and continued to ignore the two of them.

"Let's just head back home, what do you say?" Michael

suggested.

Anna nodded and took his hand. He looked down, but didn't comment on it or pull away, no matter how intense the buzzing that traveled from her palm into his was. A whole barrage of conflicting emotions tugged at him. If this was what holding her hand felt like, what would it be like to take things further? No, she was his fledgling. It was wrong to think of her as anything else.

He tried to shut down his straying mind and focused on just one thing: if she needed to hold his hand to feel safe, he owed it to her to comply. Her safety was his responsibility, after all.

Neither spoke another word as they broke into a sprint together. They didn't stop even once until they made it back to Kensington Palace Gardens and Alexander's mansion.

CHAPTER SIX

They still stood hand in hand on the gravel driveway right in front of the house when Anna came back to her senses. Their little excursion back to the *scene of the crime* had overwhelmed her. The smell of her own blood, and then the footsteps that promised her a meal thousands of times better than the raw steak she'd eaten earlier…

It was a lot to take in. And yet, she didn't want to think about any of that.

She looked down at Michael's hand, which still surrounded hers. He had made sure she hadn't done anything she would regret. As intensely thirsty as she'd felt in that strange courtyard in the city, she wasn't ready to take a life. The guilt would kill her, she was certain of it.

What a night. Although only a few hours had passed, it now felt like years ago when she'd first woken up inside the house. She was a vampire now.

Anna still could hardly believe it. She might have rejected the idea further if she hadn't felt the blood lust Lucille and Michael had been talking about. Had her eyes turned red too, like that man who had attacked her? The memory was so faint, she could just see those eyes staring at her, boring their way into her soul through the surrounding darkness.

You will come with me, the man had said. She'd heard him

clearly, but his lips had never moved. Was that the hypnosis thing Michael had been talking about earlier?

"You want to go in?" Michael asked.

Anna looked around. The gravel drive they stood on was lined by neatly kept hedges, beyond which there lay a sprawling lawn. The frost on the blades of grass sparkled in the starlight. It was magical.

Would all this make up for never seeing the sun again?

She wanted to believe so. It was too late for regrets. She glanced up at the house, with its large pillars surrounding the impressive front entrance. Above, ten windows marked the upper floor, each of them surrounded by carved stonework. Did one of these belong to the bedroom she'd woken up in? Or had hers been located toward the back?

"I have an idea," Michael said.

Anna glanced up at him and was captivated by how the soft light bounced off his chiseled cheek bones. In this light, his skin seemed to be glowing faintly. Was that how she looked too?

"What idea?" she asked, then stared at his lips, waiting for them to form a response.

He winked at her. "Trust me?"

She pressed her lips together. Should she say yes? What did she have to lose?

She nodded and was instantly whisked away, toward the side of the villa, beside a tall oak tree.

Michael jumped up into it, catching hold of the first

branch that hung at least twelve feet off the ground.

"Follow me," he said.

No way can I make that, Anna thought. But she took a deep breath and jumped, and to her surprise, found that she was hanging just next to Michael. He swung his legs up and got up on top of the thick branch, then climbed up into the next one, and then the next.

She followed right on his heels until the very top. From there, Michael leapt across to the roof of the house and turned around, waiting for her to catch up.

Anna looked down. This tree, which looked to be at least a hundred years old, was huge. She was so far off the ground, the old her would have been terrified. *I was afraid of heights,* she thought. *But now I have no more reason to be.*

She didn't hesitate anymore and jumped across the gap. It was effortless.

"That's amazing," she mumbled to herself.

Michael gestured at her to join her as he sat down on top of the ridge at the top of the roof. She did, then followed his line of sight across the front gate to the substantial villa across the road, which adjoined the park.

The view was breathtaking. She'd never seen anything like it.

In the distance, lights twinkled in the distance as they moved around the pathways in the park. Perhaps they were people out for early morning walks or cycle rides. Off to their right, Kensington Palace stood proudly in its manicured lawns, bathed in an orange-red glow. They would have turned off the main illumination of the palace as well as the other landmarks in the city hours ago, but she could still see the building clear as day thanks to what must be its emergency lighting. From here—a good 500 feet away—she could see every detail of it. Right down to the crack developing in one of the window sills on the second floor.

"Wow," she said.

Michael took her hand and pointed further ahead, to the other end of Hyde Park. "You can see the Marble Arch from here."

He was right. Although it was quite far off, the sight of it blew Anna away.

Anna pointed even further away, just more to the south. "Those lights beyond the buildings, that's what, Buckingham Palace?"

"It is indeed."

She turned to face him. "Thank you."

"Ah, forget it. I just wanted to show you the good parts of being turned. That's all."

Anna had misjudged Michael earlier. Not that he'd given her much choice. Michael hadn't shown much tact after she'd just woken up, but perhaps that wasn't his fault. This situation they found themselves in was new to the both of them.

But this little gesture of his proved that he actually did care. She'd been shaken by her experience earlier, and this had done a lot to make her feel better.

He looked over at her, letting his eyes linger on hers for a moment too long.

Anna felt a sense of familiarity now that she looked into his eyes. Like she'd seen him somewhere before, even if she had no actual recollection of it. That was silly though, obviously. Her memory or lack thereof was playing tricks on her.

She scooted a little closer to him. He wasn't so bad after all. And damn, the subdued light from the stars above made him look even more handsome. If that was even possible.

Earlier, he'd kept their eye contact to a minimum. He'd even avoided physical contact, until their outing earlier. Now, her hand rested on the roof just beside his, their little fingers touching. He didn't pull away, and neither did she.

And he continued to stare into her soul, making her heart beat faster. Was that her heart, though? Did vampires even have heartbeats?

She felt giddy and lightheaded. No matter how quickly he'd brushed it away, she was certain that this gesture meant something more than he was willing to admit.

"Do you come here often?" she asked, then grinned when she realized the cliché.

Michael smiled subtly. "Often enough to recognize a new face."

This man had an infuriatingly gorgeous smile. To go with his infuriatingly gorgeous face.

Anna's thoughts were swimming. She found it hard to focus on anything but the curve of Michael's lips.

"It's not so bad, this new life," she mumbled.

His smile widened.

She leaned in, closer and closer. His scent filled her nostrils. Intoxicating and seductive, like an expensive cologne.

Michael similarly leaned toward her until their faces were only an inch apart.

And just like that, without planning to, really, Anna pressed her lips against his.

The heartbeat in her chest seemed to speed up to a high frequency buzz. Her chest filled with—she wasn't quite sure with what. Excitement. Nerves.

Arousal.

She felt alive, like every one of her was synapses firing at an intensity she wouldn't have thought possible before. Her whole body was electric, every inch of her skin highly sensitized.

Michael reached for her, slipping his hand behind her neck and cradling her as he returned her kiss. Their tongues collided and fireworks seemed to erupt behind her closed eyelids.

It was so beautiful, she had to fight back tears.

And just like that, it was over. Michael withdrew his hand and pulled away.

Anna opened her eyes in distress. Why? Why did he stop?

"I'm sorry, this isn't fair on you," Michael stammered. He refused to look her in the eye.

Had she misread the situation completely? Had he not just brought her here to this incredibly romantic spot and showed her all the beauty that lay at their feet? Had he not just tried to convince her that immortality wasn't as scary and alien as it had seemed to be at first?

Did he not care for her?

"I'm sorry?"

"I shouldn't have done that," he said, shaking his head. "I'm your maker. It's inappropriate."

Anna didn't know what to do or where to look as he got up, dusted off his trousers, and took a few steps away from her. She'd faced rejection in the past, but nothing like this. He'd been *into* it just now, hadn't he?

"I don't understand," she mumbled, and wrapped her arms around herself protectively.

"Look." Michael reached for her shoulder, then stopped about an inch away. "I'm really sorry. I got carried away in the moment. This isn't right. I've taken advantage of your situation and I shouldn't have. This is your first night as a vampire, and you don't need to be wrapped up in all this."

Anna frowned. Taken advantage? What the hell was he talking about?

"I kissed *you*," she said. "If anyone took advantage—"

Michael shook his head. "No. I'm sorry. I'm going to go inside now. If you need anything, I'll be in the library."

Anna's throat tightened, making it impossible for her to respond. Before she had the chance to regain her composure, he'd walked across to the edge of the roof and climbed down, possibly to enter through a nearby window.

Unbelievable.

She didn't recall ever being faced with a guy acting this hot and cold around her, but then of course she wouldn't. She didn't remember much of anything.

What did it mean?

Anna pulled her legs up, wrapped her arms around them, and rested her chin on top of her knees.

A lot had happened today, and perhaps some peace and quiet was exactly what she needed. Not that it was particularly quiet up here. She could hear traffic, as well as the occasional siren, miles away. She tried to focus on the rustling of fallen leaves being carried by the odd winter breeze in the park.

That kiss, though. Holy hell. Despite the awkwardness of his sudden departure, and the confusion he left her in, she couldn't get it out of her mind.

Was everything just more intense now that she was no longer mortal? He had overwhelmed her, turned her into a mushy mess of emotions and sensations that felt completely alien. Considering she didn't have her memory back yet, this was essentially her first ever kiss now. She hated that it had to end so soon.

Although it was probably for the best. She had enough to worry already about without adding relationship issues into the mix.

If a little kiss felt this amazing, then what was sex like?

Anna groaned. She'd be a lot better off banning these speculations from her mind. He wasn't into her, or at the very least, he didn't consider her *ready*, whatever that meant.

And she wasn't about to throw herself at some guy she'd known all of what—ten hours? Most of those hours she'd been passed out. How could she even know what kind of guy he was?

Plus, she wasn't that kind of woman.

She might not remember the finer details of her old life, but she was certain of that fact.

Plus, he wasn't even into her. Or was he?

CHAPTER SEVEN

Stupid, stupid, stupid!

Michael paced restlessly around the library. No matter how much Alexander seemed to like this place for its calming influence, Michael couldn't find any peace.

He'd slipped up and given in to old habits.

Anna had hardly gotten the chance to get used to her new life, and he'd jumped in headfirst and let his cock do the thinking for him. Not only would it make things awkward going forward, it was downright inappropriate.

Michael had heard the old stories of vampires who turned women for their own pleasure, and he'd always rejected the thought. To his mind, a maker was equivalent to a father figure, or at the very least, an older sibling of sorts, making what had happened downright wrong.

He was an admirer of the female form, sure, but he wasn't underhanded or dishonest about it. He'd never forced himself on anyone.

And yet, up on the roof he'd taken advantage of his position. As her maker, he was an authority figure of sorts. Anna didn't have anyone in this new life except for him. That didn't give her much of a choice but to indulge him if he went too far.

Of course, Michael hadn't consciously tried to, but the more comfortable he'd gotten around her, the more easily he had slipped into his regular moves. She was an attractive woman, so he'd tried to seduce her. Now he couldn't forgive himself for it.

He should have known better.

The grandfather clock upstairs struck seven times, signaling that sunrise was dangerously close. He balled his fists as he left the library. As much as he wanted to stay away from Anna for a while, he couldn't risk her getting caught unaware in the sun and burn to death.

As he approached the stairs, he heard movement on the upper floor. Perhaps she'd felt the urge to head inside already. Newly made vampires had good survival instincts, though some felt the warning signs more keenly than others.

"Just making sure you're inside for sunrise," he called out.

No response.

Michael made his way up the stairs and through the hallway, only to find Anna waiting in the doorway of her room.

She averted her gaze from him. Clearly their earlier encounter had made her feel awkward too. If only he could express how sorry he was... Instead, he stood in front of her now with nothing to say.

"So I should stay here all day?" she asked, fidgeting with the bottom hem of her borrowed pullover. He took a step back, making sure to respect her personal space.

"You'll be safe in here. All the windows in this house

have blackout blinds," Michael said.

He stole a glimpse at her, top to bottom. The outfit she'd found was far from stylish, but somehow, she made it look good.

Enough with the inappropriate thoughts already!

"Oh, if you want, we could buy a few things for you to wear tomorrow… You know, until you remember where you lived before and we pick up your things," Michael suggested.

Anna shrugged. "Whatever you say."

She suppressed a yawn and went inside, shutting the door behind her without looking back even once.

What a mess. Just as Anna had finally started to warm up around him and accept the things he'd told her, he'd trampled all over her budding trust in him.

———◦◦———

Throughout the day, sleep eluded Michael, who continued to toss and turn until his body felt the arrival of dusk. He couldn't stop thinking about Anna, obviously. How she'd tried to act strong and confident, when he had first tried to explain what had happened to her. And how vulnerable she'd been once she realized she didn't have control of her new urges.

He never planned to become someone's maker, but once he no longer had a choice, he'd been determined to do the best job he could. And then of course he had betrayed his own intentions and ruined everything when he kissed her.

It should have never happened. But now that it had, he couldn't undo it, neither could he ignore the effect it had on him.

Their kiss had been unlike any he had shared with anyone before.

The pull he felt toward her was so intense, he'd found it impossible to resist her. And when their lips connected, it had released a whole host of alien feelings within him.

He loved women and had bedded so many over the years that he had lost count. But he wasn't a selfish lover; what he loved the most during any of his encounters was the pleasure he was able to give to his partners. Those special little things he could do that human men couldn't.

A woman's face signaling the peak of her orgasm was the most rewarding thing he'd ever seen, and it was those moments that he'd kept chasing during the past three decades of his renewed life. His own physical satisfaction had always been an afterthought.

But with Anna, during that short kiss, he'd felt something deeper and more primal. He'd felt the need to make her his. And he also felt like a pervert for it.

Never before had he felt any desire to possess a woman.

How could he face her now? How could he keep himself in check as they trained her new abilities? She had so much to learn, and nobody else to teach her.

On his bedside table, his phone came to life and started

to ring.

Michael leaned across and read the caller ID. Alexander.

"Yes?" he answered.

"Just checking in. Lucille had left me a message. Has she been by the house?" Alexander said.

Michael closed his eyes. "Yes, she's investigating the rogue vampires who attacked Anna."

"Anna?"

"Yes, that's her name. She's suffering from memory loss, but she remembered that much."

An awkward silence followed. "Look, I wanted to apologize for my reaction earlier," Alexander started.

Michael shook his head. "It's all right. Since I have you on the line, I might as well tell you how things went last night. You know she didn't even believe me she'd been turned at first? It took quite a bit of convincing."

"Interesting. You sound strange, is everything all right?" Alexander asked.

Michael took a deep breath. "Actually… I suppose I owe it to you to say it out loud. This whole business of becoming someone's maker has turned out to be quite the headache."

"How so?"

Michael frowned. Was Alexander genuinely asking or could he detect a hint of Schadenfreude in his voice?

"She's… she's a handful."

"So were you."

"This is different." Michael sighed.

"Perhaps you don't realize how difficult you were."

Alexander wasn't getting it, obviously. How could he? But who else was there to ask for advice?

"Actually, *she* isn't strictly the problem. Not since she started believing me. But I fear I may have betrayed her trust and I don't know how to recover from that."

Alexander paused for a moment before responding. "What exactly do you mean *betrayed her trust?*"

"I kissed her." Michael turned onto his side and covered his eyes with his free hand. Although they'd been through a lot together, Alexander and he, this was still embarrassing to admit.

"So? Did she not like it?" Alexander asked.

Michael was stunned by his reaction. "What? That's not the point. I abused my position. I crossed the line! I'm her maker, for God's sake!"

"Honestly, when you first came home with her I had trouble understanding your reasoning. All I could see were risks. Perhaps you didn't just want to save her out of the goodness of your heart—perhaps something else motivated you?"

"Really; *that's* what you think of me?" Michael couldn't believe his ears. He had his flaws, like any man or vampire did. But he wasn't that deplorable. Did Alexander really think he would go out of his way to bring home some woman to be his concubine?

"Don't misunderstand me. I'm not judging you. I have

my vices just as you have yours. Answer me this: how did it happen? The kiss, I mean."

Michael did his best to suppress his outrage at Alexander's earlier statement and thought back to last night. "It had been a difficult few hours until she finally believed a word I was telling her. In fact I believe what finally convinced her was when she first felt actually thirsty. Lucille and I had to restrain her or she would have hunted down a nearby human. Once we got back, she was despondent about losing control, so I took her up onto the roof."

"Your special place. Remember how many nights you used to spend up there when you were newly turned?" Alexander reminisced.

Michael nodded. "Yes. Well, I thought it might help her gain some perspective. We sat together, admiring the view. Then it happened."

"You like her."

"What? Now you're just being ridiculous! I don't—" Michael protested.

"Think about it! How many women, vampire or human, have you taken up to the roof?"

Michael didn't even need time to think. The answer was simple. "None."

"Exactly. That's the point I was trying to make. Your other reason for wanting to save her life. You felt something when you first saw her."

So that was what Alexander had meant. It made sense

for him to draw those conclusions, especially since he had found Cat to share his life with. Michael's own thoughts had gone in an entirely different direction. "Right. Well, I still don't think it appropriate for me, as her maker, to—"

"Will you stop? From what you're telling me, this woman seems to know her own mind very well. If you did anything wrong, she would have reacted accordingly. She is your equal now. She could have defended herself."

Michael shook his head. He'd seen Alexander with Lucille and Julius. They had their flaws, but they were a family, with distinct roles.

"Would you have ever kissed Lucille like that?" Michael asked.

"Why would you—no, she's my sister!"

"Exactly my point. And Julius, would he ever have seduced Lucille?"

"Michael, this comparison does not stand. You are not Julius and Anna is not Lucille."

"Why not? I'm her maker. She is my fledgling."

Alexander sighed on the other end of the line. "There is a difference. The dynamic between Julius, Lucille, and me is unique to our situation. Julius made us as his children, hence he set the tone for our relationship. You're creating a big moral dilemma where there isn't one. If you like her, and she likes you, then what's the problem?"

Michael shook his head again. He wasn't ready to accept it. Even if Alexander's perception was much more relaxed, Michael's wasn't. A maker was a maker, and a lover was a lover. He wouldn't accept a crossover between the two. The more he thought about it, the bigger the knot in his chest. It was wrong. Immoral.

"My friend, stop worrying so much," Alexander said. "The most important thing right now is for you to calm down and focus on Anna's training. Get her to bring her impulses under control so Cat and I can come home, and worry about everything else later."

Finally Alexander said something Michael could agree with. "Okay. I'll do my best."

"I know you will."

"I'll be in touch." Michael sighed as he hung up the call.

Alexander was right; Anna's training was the most important thing right now. Nobody—least of all Alexander—had ever said this was going to be easy.

Michael got out of bed and listened for any sounds elsewhere in the house. Nothing. If he hurried, he could go out and get Anna some real food. Once she was satisfied, they'd start working on desensitizing her to human activity.

CHAPTER EIGHT

Anna woke up with the overwhelming metallic scent of blood in her nose. It had entered her room and tickled her nostrils, dragging her against her will from the deepest slumber. She didn't recall what she'd been dreaming of, just that the color red had entered her mind barely a moment before she'd become alert.

Now that she sat up straight in bed, she was even more aware of it. It was irresistible.

She quickly put on a robe and rushed out of her room.

The hallway was empty.

Within moments, she had found her way down the stairs all the way to the library. Inside, Lucille and Michael were already waiting.

"Are you thirsty?" Michael asked, raising one of those same antique crystal glasses from last night toward her. It was filled with the most beautiful deep red liquid Anna had ever seen.

"Is that..." She didn't finish her sentence, just inhaled, and was instantly hit by a bout of lightheadedness.

"Blood," Lucille said in her usual monotone voice. The woman couldn't be more unpleasant if she tried.

Anna ignored her and headed straight for Michael, accepting the glass and gazing down into it. Her own reflection in blood red greeted her, along with swirls of black shadows which gave the impression that the glass was a lot deeper than it actually was. It was as though the liquid had sucked the light out of all of its surroundings, like a black hole, and the sight was both exciting as well as terrifying. It attracted Anna like a moth to a flame.

She had no control over it.

Without thinking about it any further, she put the glass to her lips and drank. The second the stuff hit her lips, she was in heaven. The high was intense, like she imagined certain drugs might have been. It was unlike anything she'd ever experienced.

Now oblivious to her surroundings, Anna gulped all of it down until the glass was empty. Her eyes were closed, not that she'd consciously closed them. She stood still and enjoyed the rush that passed through every part of her body. This was the pinnacle of pleasure. Better than an orgasm, better than last night's raw steak, better than the best Belgian chocolate, better than even that absolutely wonderful expensive brandy she'd tasted the night before.

She wasn't sure how long she'd been standing in ecstasy with the empty glass in her hand. By the time she opened her eyes, she found that Lucille looked even more bored than she had before, and Michael had started studying his mobile phone.

Weird, watching a vampire doing something that natural and seemingly human.

And where was *her* phone? That would give her some clues regarding her old life, surely.

"She's back," Lucille observed.

Anna ignored her and focused on Michael instead. Their kiss, followed by his sudden rejection, had confused her deeply. Now that the effects of the blood were starting to wear off, the embarrassment and awkwardness she'd felt last night returned with a vengeance.

Michael looked up without making proper eye contact. "Wonderful. Now that you've fed, we can consider going out."

Lucille got up and folded her arms. "We've received some tips which could possibly point to your attackers."

Anna turned to face her. "Where are they hiding?"

Lucille shrugged. "That remains to be seen. But there has been some suspicious activity around the derelict power station in Chelsea."

Chelsea? That was a very upmarket part of the city. Why would anyone want to start trouble there of all places?

Michael put his phone in his pocket. "Very well, let's investigate."

Anna hesitated. Was it a good idea for her to go out and possibly end up attacking some random passerby like what had almost happened last night?

"Ready?" Michael asked.

Anna hesitated and scanned the room. Lucille had already left, leaving the two of them alone. "Wouldn't it be risky for me to come?"

He shook his head and smiled at her briefly. "You've fed on human blood now. It'll be fine. The first step to resisting temptation is to feed regularly."

That was *human blood?* Anna wasn't sure how to feel about that. Sure, it was her natural source of food now, but the thought still freaked her out a bit. Someone had been hurt and made to bleed to feed her.

"Don't worry, they didn't feel a thing, nor will they remember," Michael said.

Anna looked up at him. When their eyes met, she could see nothing but warmth in his. Perhaps he really did care. But then why had he rejected her last night?

"Fine. Let's go," she said.

It didn't take the three vampires long to reach Chelsea by cab. And despite the close proximity of the human driver, Anna was able to keep her urges under control. Michael was right. That glass of blood she drank before setting off had made all the difference.

How often did vampires need to feed to stay in control? This was just one of the many questions she still had about her new reality. Hopefully she'd get the chance to speak to Michael in private at some point, without Lucille's presence adding to the awkwardness.

"So this is it," Lucille said as she pointed to the fenced off industrial complex. Large chimneys on all corners of the building towered over their little group.

On the road, cars and pedestrians passed them by, oblivious to the potential danger. They were three vampires, among a sea of humans, and yet they managed to blend in perfectly.

Michael scanned the fence. "Let's find a way in. There are too many onlookers for us to simply jump across."

Lucille nodded and marched down the road, while Michael and Anna inspected the perimeter of the lot in the opposite direction.

Anna tried to do her bit, but she found it hard to focus. There were still so many scents in the air that tried to pull her in all directions. It had been easy enough to see the variety in the human population before she'd been turned, but only now did Anna realize just how varied their scents were. It was almost like being faced with a colorful buffet, in which every dish looked and smelled more appealing than the one that came before.

"I've found it," Michael whispered. He'd spoken just loud enough that Lucille had heard him from the other end of the street, but quiet enough that none of the humans had noticed.

Anna tried her best to drag herself away from all the distractions and joined Michael in front of an innocuous breach in the chain link fence. He stepped aside and allowed Anna to enter first.

Lucille followed, and finally the three of them were inside the abandoned yard in front of the old power plant.

It was obvious that it had been out of use for a long time. The yard was overgrown with weeds and had been used as a dump to discard unwanted household appliances and other garbage. Still, the place had a strange beauty to it which Anna probably would have never noticed as a human.

She gazed up to the roof of the abandoned power station. How amazing would it be to climb all the way to the top of one of those chimneys? The views would be amazing from up there.

From the corner of Anna's eye, she saw Lucille approach the front of the building, where one of the previously barricaded doors had been broken open. Inside, a shadow moved past the opening, startling Anna.

"There's someone in there," she whispered, pointing at the entrance.

"Probably a squatter," Michael remarked.

"But if those vampires are hiding here…" Anna wondered aloud.

"Vampires would never let themselves be seen so easily. They're probably long gone by now."

Anna hoped he was right, but still kept a distance behind Michael, as the two of them followed Lucille inside. It would take some time for her to become as fearless as her two companions.

Although it was pretty dark inside, Anna could see her surroundings in astounding detail. Indeed, there were some people inside, squatters like Michael had assumed. A few of them had made beds for themselves using cardboard, newspapers, and discarded clothes.

Lucille ignored them and walked further into the

building, but Anna caught a whiff of something she couldn't ignore.

The scent was so familiar, and yet she couldn't place where she'd last smelled it. She followed it to an empty squat. After she pushed some newspapers aside with her foot, she found what she was looking for. A plain black messenger bag. *Her* bag; she was sure of it.

"I don't believe it," Anna muttered as she picked it up.

It looked slightly worse for the wear, but she recognized the way it felt to the touch, the scuffs on the buckle that had developed over time, and even the nearly invisible coffee stain on the strap.

Michael appeared by her side. "What is it?"

"This." Anna turned and held up the bag. "This is mine."

Michael leaned forward to inspect it. "It has your scent."

Anna's heart was beating faster. Would the contents of this bag help her figure out more about her life? Only one way to find out.

She opened it and found that it was mostly empty. No wallet, no phone. If those things had still been in there when the bag was found by whoever's squat this was, they were long gone by now. She rummaged around inside. There were just some chocolate wrappers and a pack of tissues.

Then she found the zip to the inner compartment. Inside was a solitary business card. She picked it up and almost instinctively held it to her nose. Yes, this was unmistakably hers.

She remembered the moment she'd first received the stack of fresh new business cards from the printer.

Anna felt Michael's eyes still on her as she turned the card over, revealing the most important clue yet:

Anna James Catering

Underneath, there was a phone number as well as a website address, though unfortunately, no physical address.

"Where are the two of you? I found something significant," Lucille's voice called out from somewhere much deeper inside the building.

Anna and Michael shared a quick look. This trip had already paid off as far as Anna was concerned. Who knew what other clues lurked in the depths of this abandoned industrial complex.

They joined Lucille, who had found what looked like some sort of control room. Inside, she was poring over old blueprints of the facility, pointing to the center of it. "There. If I were a newcomer in this city, and I was up to something I wouldn't want to draw attention to, that's where I'd do it."

Michael leaned forward and also studied the plans, but Anna couldn't take her eyes off her old business card.

It wasn't as pristine as in her memory. Something had changed, but she couldn't put her finger on what it was.

She cleared her throat. "I think I'd like some time alone to think," she told Michael, as Lucille looked on with one eyebrow raised.

"That's understandable," he said, glancing over at Lucille. "I'll take you home then."

Lucille rolled her eyes, but didn't say anything.

"No, no, I'll just take a cab back," Anna mumbled. "It'll be fine." It had to be, right? She'd been able to control herself on the journey here, so why would the way back be any different? She couldn't expect Michael to babysit her wherever she went; she'd lose her mind.

"I must insist. I'll accompany you."

Lucille put one hand on her hip and shook her head. "Michael, I understand that you've got a shiny new toy, but this is important. We're not done here yet."

Did Lucille honestly just refer to her as a *toy?* Anna couldn't believe her ears.

"Excuse me?" Anna snapped.

"You're new to this, I understand," Lucille started, then glanced across at Michael. "But believe me, I know his type very well. His dedication will wear off once another woman catches his eye. You might as well learn to stand on your own two feet early on."

"I'm not—I mean, things aren't like that!" Anna protested. Why bother, though. Who did Lucille think she was, anyway? She didn't know the first thing about what kind of person Anna was; she'd never allow herself to be used like that. Not that it was any of Lucille's business.

Michael crossed his arms as he faced Lucille. "Before you disrespect me, you might want to consider whether or not you want my cooperation in your little investigation."

Lucille shrugged. "I can just have Julius summon you and compel you to help me. It makes no difference to me. But remember that you're on shaky ground with him already."

Michael glared at her, and Lucille glared back.

Anna, meanwhile, turned away from the two riled up vampires and left. She didn't care what these two got up to next, she was going back to the house to research her own past. That was her priority. Nothing and no one would be able to stop her.

CHAPTER NINE

Anna had every intention of heading straight back to the mansion when she left the derelict lot. She'd even hailed a cab and started to talk to the driver, when some peculiar new sensation overwhelmed her. The more she spoke with him and made eye contact with him, the more she felt a strange new presence in her mind. He was in there with her, or was she in his mind with him? It was hard to tell the difference.

"Say, do you have a phone?" Anna asked the man.

"Sure, love," the cabbie responded, his voice monotone, as though he didn't realize what he was saying.

"Show me." Anna stretched out her hand. "You don't mind if I borrow it for a bit, do you?"

The man didn't hesitate, just handed his device over. "Not at all. Glad to help."

Anna smiled at him and opened the rear door of the cab, taking a seat inside. "Just wait here for a bit, I'll let you know where I want to go in a second," she said.

So this was the hypnosis thing Michael had been talking about. It was a lot easier than she'd thought. In fact it came almost completely naturally to her. No way was a hardened London cabbie going to hand his phone to just anyone who asked for it. She could have so easily stolen it; not that she was planning to.

Anna held her breath as she typed in the website address from her old business card. It was basic, just a couple of pages of information, but no address. She read through the whole thing, studying it in detail. Slowly, memories of herself writing these words came back to her. She'd been full of excitement and hope at the time. Setting up her own catering business had been a longtime dream.

Something wasn't quite right, though, as though that memory had been tainted by a negative event.

It hadn't been a success, she thought. *I couldn't make it work.* A sense of disappointment filled her chest, as though she'd just now made the decision to give up on the business.

She looked down at the card, with its dog-eared corner and slightly faded text. She'd started off with a stack of 200 brand new business cards and this was the only one she had left.

And since the website hadn't pointed her to her home address, this clue seemed to be a dead end.

Anna looked up through the side window. The small shops on the other side of the road didn't look familiar. Her bag just happened to end up inside that building. As far as she knew, she'd never been here before.

"Just take me to Kensington Palace Gardens like I said," Anna instructed the cabbie.

She handed him his phone back through the coin slot in the Plexiglass partition between them.

"As you wish, dear." He started the engine and pulled out into traffic.

Anna sat back and listlessly looked out the window. This had been a waste of time. The memories she'd gained had only brought her down.

What would she have done in the past to cheer herself up? Anna closed her eyes and tried to remember. It was like all of her memories were right there inside of her head, but something was blocking them and keeping them from her.

Chocolate.

Anna opened her eyes. The scent hung heavy in the air. Molten chocolate. Hints of vanilla and cinnamon, and the smell of freshly baked wheat tying it all together.

"Pull over here, will you?" she said.

The cabbie did as asked.

She rummaged around in her pockets for money to pay him, but there was none. In her eagerness to start investigating the business card, she'd forgotten to ask Michael for some. "How much do I owe you?" she asked.

The cabbie turned around and smiled at her. "This one's on the house, love."

Anna smiled back at him. She could really get used to this hypnosis business. "Thank you so much. You've been very helpful."

He just kept on looking at her with a vague smile on his face. *Now what?* Was he just going to hang around here, stuck in a trance?

"You best be on your way back to where you picked me up and wait for your next fare," Anna said.

He nodded and put his hands back on the steering wheel.

Whew. She didn't want to consider the possibility of this man hanging around here endlessly, waiting for her like a lost puppy.

Anna got out of the cab. It pulled away almost immediately after she shut the door.

Now that she was outside, those familiar scents she'd just picked up on had only intensified. She started to follow her nose up the street, dodging other pedestrians, until she felt compelled to turn off into a smaller street.

The cobbled street underfoot felt familiar. This was a part of the city where she'd spent a lot of time in the past. She continued on, zigzagging through the tighter streets until she had reached her destination.

The shiny, modern building stood out starkly against the historic buildings all around. This bakery had been a part of her walk to and from work for quite a while. Being back here provided a sense of belonging and nostalgia.

She looked around, hoping for further clues. Which way was home?

Anna then closed her eyes and tried to figure it out by scent. The sweet aromas emanating from the bakery covered everything else. She simply couldn't make out what was under them.

But Anna wasn't easily discouraged. Instead of giving up, she started to systematically walk through the streets surrounding the bakery in a grid pattern. Sooner or later, she would see something familiar, she was sure of it.

This went on for ten minutes or so, until she inadvertently walked into an alley with a dead end. The graffiti covered buildings surrounding her seemed abandoned; broken windows marked the upper floors, some of which were boarded up. No way was this place going to provide clues as to where she lived.

Anna was about to turn around and continue to explore the neighborhood, when a tall, slender figure materialized in front of her.

"Will you look at that," the man said.

He looked old; just how old, Anna couldn't be sure. His skin was papery and almost translucent. His deep black eyes stood out starkly against his otherwise faded appearance.

"Do I know you?" Anna stammered. She could barely stand looking at the man. The moment she made eye contact, it felt like the man's hand had penetrated her chest and started to squeeze at her heart. It was painful, terrifying, otherworldly.

He approached her and looked her over top to bottom like one might inspect cattle at an auction.

"This is unexpected, to say the least."

Curiosity had brought her here, but Anna was over that now. She wanted desperately to run, yet her feet refused to move.

"Who are you?" she tried again.

The man smiled, revealing an entire row of razor sharp

teeth. His longer canines gave him away as a vampire, but the rest of him was unlike what Anna had seen in Michael or even Lucille. He didn't look entirely normal, even for a vampire.

Anna opened her mouth to question him further, but she was unable to make a sound.

"Take her." The man stood back and waited as two figures, entirely dressed in black, flitted out of the windows above and flanked Anna.

She tried to turn around to leave, but they had grabbed her by the arms so tightly she couldn't move at all. Within seconds, a hood of some sort ended up on her head, cutting off her vision completely. Even in this new form, she felt as helpless as a human would have been.

They lifted her up and started to carry her, presumably into the building they'd just come from. The only senses Anna had left were smell and sound. Wherever they were taking her, it smelled damp and moldy, as though someone had discarded a lot of rubbish here and left it to rot. Occasionally, the ammonia-laden scent of urine overpowered everything else.

She could hear doors open and close, as well as echoes of the same. But her assailants were so light on their feet that she couldn't hear their movements at all. Not a single footstep, neither a breath nor heartbeat. They were silent as death. The only sounds she could hear were the ambient noises of the city: traffic, sirens, the deep rumble of the occasional underground train.

Michael had explained that vampires didn't harm other vampires, so these must be the rogues that had attacked her in the first place. It was the only logical explanation; that was why their leader had recognized her. In trying to locate evidence of her old life, she'd been discovered by the very creatures she'd tried to escape.

The further they carried her, the quieter her surroundings became, until she couldn't even hear the traffic anymore.

Finally, they pushed her forward into an empty space and shut a heavy door behind her. Anna clawed at the hood on her face and tore it off as quickly as she could.

The view that greeted her was unexpected; the room was narrow and long, with a curved ceiling like a tunnel, but there was nothing at the end of it, just a solid wall. The only way out was the heavy metal door that she'd just heard shut behind her. She still couldn't hear a single sound other than her own breaths and movements.

Where was she?

———◆———

They had overpowered her so easily. Despite her changed form, formidable strength, and additional powers, she was helpless to stop her captors this second time around, either. Anna found herself alone in the dark, cut off from the outside world. The walls surrounding her were thick and solid. She'd found as much as she'd explored them by touch.

How long she'd been in here? She wasn't quite sure. Every so often a deep vibration rocked the walls around her—a tube train, perhaps?

Yesterday she'd felt the sunrise just before it happened. She couldn't explain it really, but it had compelled her to get off the roof just in time. She didn't feel that way yet, so it still had to be dark outside. Or perhaps she was so far away from the sun that she wouldn't be able to feel the coming of dawn.

The darkness wasn't as disorienting as it would have been to a human; what bothered her more was that her brand new super sensitive hearing couldn't pick up on anything useful either. Her five senses were useless to her now. Although she tried her best to stay calm, the walls seemed to want to close in on her.

"Let me out!" she screamed.

There was no response, just her own dull echo.

"People will be coming to look for me!"

It was no use. Either they weren't within earshot, or they were ignoring her.

For the first time in two days, she was completely and utterly alone.

Michael would come to look for her, though, wouldn't he? Then again, she hadn't gone home like she'd told him. So how would he even find her here?

She sank down onto the ground, resting her back against the cold concrete wall, and wrapped her arms around herself. She had nothing and no one right now, only what was in her thoughts.

It wouldn't be helpful to worry about whether Michael could track her down somehow, so she diverted her attention to something else. Their relationship.

As distasteful as Lucille's remarks had been, some of what she'd said could explain why Michael had rejected her after she'd kissed him.

If he wasn't the committed relationship type, then getting into some kind of romantic relationship with a woman he'd just turned into a vampire would be the last thing he'd want. She had nowhere else to go. She didn't even remember where she lived before he took her home.

So if they ended up together, he'd be stuck with her in the same house. That would be beyond awkward.

Of course he hadn't reciprocated her kiss.

How stupid and naive she'd been.

He hadn't wanted her dead—that was why he'd saved her. And he'd been trying to teach her about what it meant to be a vampire, because he felt responsible for her safety now. But he didn't want anything more than that.

Why would he? He was immortal, and he could hypnotize any woman in the world to be with him. Why would he want to tie himself to some newbie who had willingly walked into a bloody trap and let herself be captured by the same people who had tried to kill her in the first place?

Ugh. She'd been so reckless and stupid. Instead of getting out of that cab to investigate this neighborhood, she should have gone home and come back to this area with Michael later.

As awkward as it felt to admit it to herself, she should have asked for help.

Anna rested her head on her knees and closed her eyes.

Her future was out of her hands now. All she could do was wait.

CHAPTER TEN

———◆———

Michael was furious. How dare Lucille disrespect him like that in front of Anna? What business did she have, meddling in their relationship?

Of course, he'd had no choice but to stay behind as Anna left, because Lucille was right. Julius would have very little patience for him if he didn't cooperate with a Council investigation. And so he was even more frustrated.

Why did Lucille need him for this, though? They didn't get along, and he hadn't even seen the rogue vampires who had created this mess. He had no further intel to share. What use could she possibly have for him?

At the same time, he worried about Anna finding her way back home on her own. The blood she'd drank earlier should keep her from doing anything rash, but you really never knew with a young vampire like her. In his first days, he had raised a whole lot of hell on his own. If the likes of Lucille and Julius had found out about all his transgressions from back in the day, he probably would have been put to death.

She was his responsibility. Not just to make sure she didn't attack anyone, but also for her own safety. If the vampires who had attacked her found her wandering around the city alone, they might see her as a threat.

The more he thought about them, the angrier Lucille's

remarks made him.

"You had no business talking to her like that," Michael finally said.

Lucille stopped inspecting the large incinerator she'd identified as a perfect vampire hiding place.

"What?"

"That I'd move on to someone else. I'm her maker. That's not something I'm willing to take lightly."

"Her maker. Right." Lucille shook her head and climbed inside the hatch.

Michael didn't move. Just because she was in there didn't mean he had to follow. "What are you trying to say?"

Lucille stuck her head out and glared at him. "I've walked this earth a lot longer than the likes of you."

"That doesn't give you the right to convince my fledgling that I'm going to just abandon her at will."

"What exactly is your problem? That I advised her to be independent or that I told her the truth about what you are? In any case, I thought you'd welcome the help. Nobody likes a clingy fledgling."

"It wasn't your place. And you have no idea *who* I am," Michael corrected her.

Lucille rolled her eyes. "So you like her. Whatever. Now, if you'll stop arguing for a moment, come see this."

"I don't *like* her! I'm responsible for her. There's a difference!"

Michael swallowed his anger and approached the hatch.

It was no wonder she'd roped him into this stupid investigation. Anyone as abrasive as Lucille probably didn't have very many allies, and certainly no friends.

What vampire in their right mind would want to befriend the Council Enforcer anyway? It was much too risky to keep that kind of company.

"What is it?" he asked impatiently.

She pointed at the deep gashes on the inside of the hatch. "What do you think?"

"How would I know? Someone scratched the door?"

"Someone was locked in here and tried to fight his way out." Lucille smiled to herself.

Michael frowned. Her reality was vastly different from his own, if this gruesome discovery actually pleased her this much.

"These marks are quite deep. A human couldn't have done this," Lucille remarked as she followed the gashes in the reinforced metal. "Someone locked a vampire in here."

Lucille climbed out of the incinerator and wandered off with a spring in her step. Michael remained, scratching his head. She was unnervingly cheerful. Looking at the marks Lucille had just inspected, he felt horrified, not excited.

He was about to comment on her bizarre behavior when a sharp pain pierced his chest. *What the hell?*

He closed his eyes, just as a second bout of pain and horror hit him. They had made a terrible discovery, but that was no reason to have a visceral reaction like this. Something horrible was happening somewhere else, he just knew it.

"Lucille," he called out as he stumbled out of the same hatch.

"Lucille!"

"What?" Her voice was muffled.

"Something is wrong!" Michael said.

Lucille returned to his position and scrutinized him.

He found it hard to explain what was happening, so he just gestured at his own chest. "I feel something. Here."

She cocked her head to the side and frowned. "You feel the Bond?"

"The what?"

"The Bond. The connection between maker and newborn. Is something wrong with her?"

"How would I know, I've never been anyone's maker before!" Michael argued. *Shit.* Was that what he was feeling? Was Anna in danger? He really shouldn't have let her out of his sight.

"What exactly is it that you feel?" Lucille asked.

"Like someone is trying to tear my chest open and rip my heart out." It sounded overly dramatic now that he'd said it out loud. But it was still the most accurate description he could come up with.

"We should go." Lucille didn't give him the chance to respond before grabbing him by the arm and dragging him out of the building at superhuman speed.

Outside, Michael could breathe better, but he was still overcome by dread.

She pulled her phone out of her pocket and started tapping away at it. "The house seems secure."

"You're surveilling Alexander's house now?" Michael asked, as he looked over her shoulder at the various video feeds on her screen.

Lucille glanced at him sideways. "After what happened, Julius didn't exactly give me another choice."

That's how she'd known about Anna's arrival. And here he'd thought Gillian or some other disgruntled vampire had taken it upon themselves to spy on them. This made a lot more sense.

"So if the house is fine, then where is Anna?" Michael wondered aloud.

"What if she never made it home?" Lucille asked.

"Where else would she have gone? She doesn't remember much from before the Ritual. Not even where she lived." As soon as Michael had finished talking, he started to doubt his own words.

"Perhaps she remembered something," Lucille offered.

Michael nodded. That was possible. Her memory had slowly been coming back.

"So how do we find her?" Michael asked.

Lucille didn't answer, neither did she stop walking. They returned to the gap in the fence and climbed through it. Lucille led the way toward some shops further up the road. Except for a restaurant and a small supermarket, the rest of the shops had already closed for the night.

"What are you thinking? How do we find her?" Michael

repeated himself.

Lucille pointed at the parked cars, one of them a black cab. "Good old fashioned canvassing."

Michael frowned. Anna had left over half an hour ago. What were the chances that this guy knew anything? Lucille's idea was better than nothing, though.

As they got closer to the cab, Michael examined the driver. He was just sitting there, with both hands on the steering, looking straight ahead. All the other people around here were going about their usual business: talking on the phone, checking their watches as they rushed on by carrying bags of groceries.

This guy was doing nothing at all, and yet he didn't even look bored.

Lucille knocked on his window, but he didn't react.

"He's been hypnotized," Michael observed.

Lucille turned and shot him a disapproving look. "You taught her how to hypnotize people already? Why would you do that? She doesn't even know how to feed herself yet!"

Michael raised his hands in defense. "I did nothing of the sort! She must have figured it out on her own."

Although hypnosis was a talent all vampires possessed, it didn't come easily to most fledglings. Anna really was something special, and he couldn't help but feel a sense of pride. This wasn't the time to dwell on how special or how talented Anna was, though.

She was in danger, and this human was their best

possible lead.

Michael approached the driver's side window of the cab and knocked on it again. "We need your help." His tone was firm as he spoke, and his focus was entirely aimed at infiltrating the man's mind with his own. He was quite young in vampire terms himself, but he also had somewhat of a talent for mind control.

Sure enough, the cabbie turned his head and looked Michael directly in the eye. "Of course, what do you need?"

"Did you pick up a woman from here earlier— curvaceous, wavy, dark blond hair, and light brown eyes? Where did you drop her?"

The driver frowned and his eyes went distant again, as though he was reliving the moment. "We were going to Kensington Palace Gardens, when suddenly she made me pull over. I was going to wait for her, but she told me to head back here and wait for my next fare."

Michael and Lucille exchanged a look. That's why she'd never made it home. But what had inspired her to abandon the idea of heading back to the house?

"Can you take us there?" Michael asked.

The cabbie smiled and nodded. "Of course. Happy to help."

Michael opened the rear door of the cab for Lucille, and then joined her inside.

"I can't believe a newborn could have done this," Lucille grumbled. "I've been in this city a long time, and cab drivers have always been some of the most suspicious and difficult humans I've had the displeasure of dealing with."

Michael looked out the window as the taxi pulled into the road and suppressed a sigh. One needed people skills in order to deal with difficult humans, something which Lucille sorely lacked.

"I suppose she's not just any other newborn," Michael remarked, mostly to himself.

"We shall see." Lucille folded her arms and looked out the window at her side.

Michael glanced at her, then shook his head. He'd never understand Lucille. Was she jealous of Anna? Did she dislike her for some reason? Or was this just her default behavior?

They sat in silence as the cab zipped through the dense traffic of the city, until it came to a halt somewhere on Cromwell Road, which was particularly busy.

The cabbie turned around to face them. "This is it."

Michael nodded and grabbed for his wallet. "How much?"

"Oh, I must have forgotten to switch on the meter. It's fine. I hope you two find what you're looking for."

Michael focused his thoughts again, this time aiming to release the mental connection between himself and the driver. That was where Anna must have gone wrong; that was why the man had still been under her spell even after he'd dropped her off. He'd teach her how to do it properly, if only he could find her and take her to safety first.

As soon as they got out, Lucille started to walk.

"What have you got?" Michael asked, as he caught up with her.

"She was here," Lucille said as she scanned the street ahead. "Her trail is still fresh."

Michael inhaled deeply, but he couldn't pick out Anna's scent in the muddled chaos that surrounded them. Shops, cafés, restaurants, and crowds of people confused his senses.

He understood now; Lucille was a talented tracker. That was what made her so valuable to the Council.

She didn't seem to have any difficulty picking out Anna's scent, and started to walk again.

They continued up the road for a little bit, and then turned off into a smaller side street.

Lucille paused for a moment at the next intersection. "It gets confusing here," she mumbled.

Michael looked around. None of the surrounding buildings or streets seemed particularly interesting. And yet there must have been something here to attract Anna's attention.

"She's been in all of these streets," Lucille said. "Almost like she's been walking around in circles and doubling back on herself."

"She was looking for something," Michael concluded.

Lucille nodded. "It'll take too long if we rely on my

sense of smell alone. It's your turn."

Michael raised an eyebrow.

"Follow the Bond," she urged.

Michael closed his eyes; doing so seemed to strengthen his connection to Anna. Although he could still feel that something was very wrong, he couldn't easily pinpoint where the feeling originated. It didn't help that in closing his eyes, he kept *seeing* her. The way she looked at him up on the roof, just before they'd kissed. It broke his heart to consider the possibility that he might never see her again.

"I can't tell where she is," he said.

"Try harder!" Lucille said.

Michael opened his eyes and glared at her. "I am! It's not that easy."

Lucille observed him for a moment, then pursed her lips. "Okay, I have an idea. Close your eyes again."

Michael did as asked, and almost instantly, Lucille started dragging him forward by his arm. "You just let me know if we're getting warmer or colder,"

Michael was about to protest that this wasn't a game, when suddenly he felt it. The tension in his chest seemed to grow marginally. "Okay, warmer."

CHAPTER ELEVEN

It didn't take Michael and Lucille all that long to locate the spot where Michael's connection to Anna was the strongest. There was just one problem: they'd ended up in the center of a cobbled road with no sign of Anna anywhere.

The buildings surrounding them looked innocuous enough, but every time they approached one of them, Michael's sixth sense suggested that Anna wasn't inside.

"What if she's underneath us?" Michael kneeled down and placed his hand flat on the cold ground. Sure enough, he could sense her more keenly from there.

There was a manhole cover near their position which wouldn't be difficult for even one vampire to lift up.

"She could be in the sewer," Michael said.

"That's not all that's down there," Lucille said. "London has a very extensive system of tunnels. That would explain why these buildings don't feel right to you."

Michael nodded. It made sense. He picked up the heavy metal disk and cast it aside, then he jumped down into the darkness below, landing squarely on his feet in a puddle.

The water didn't take long to penetrate his shoes and the legs of his trousers. Ordinarily, getting soaked in human filth would annoy the hell out of him. But if he found Anna and stopped the terrible threat that seemed to loom over her, it was worth the sacrifice.

The only problem was that he still couldn't pick up on her scent down here. The stench of human excrement and garbage was too overwhelming.

Lucille landed next to him and marched straight ahead. Perhaps her nose had picked up something his couldn't.

They continued for ten, twenty feet, then Lucille stopped in her tracks.

"Listen," she said.

Michael shook his head. He couldn't hear a thing.

"We better go," she whispered.

Before he could question her, or they could retreat, Michael saw why Lucille had become spooked all of a sudden. The two vampires that appeared before them looked very different from any Michael had seen before. Their eyes glowed in the dark as they bared their sharp fangs.

"You shouldn't be here," the one on the left hissed.

"This is our domain," the other said.

"We made a mistake, our apologies," Lucille said, trying to placate them.

Michael shot her a confused look. This didn't sound at all like the Lucille he knew and disliked. What had gotten into her?

Anna was here somewhere. Couldn't Lucille just tell these two what was what, that they were breaking Council laws by holding one of their own? Couldn't they fight these two idiots?

Michael opened his mouth, but Lucille rested her hand on his arm to silence him. They exchanged a look and he decided against better judgement to follow her lead. The safety of his fledgling was on the line, but she had been in the business of enforcing Council law much longer than he'd even been alive. Perhaps she knew best.

"What's your business here?" the other vampire asked.

Both of them stood slightly hunched forward with their fists balled, ready to fight if necessary.

"We were just looking for a place to stash prey. You know how it is." Lucille gestured at the tunnel surrounding them. "But seeing as this spot is taken, we'll be on our way."

The two rogue vampires exchanged a look, then surged forward.

Lucille took Michael's hand and dragged him back toward the manhole they'd entered from. They fled as quickly as they could, jumped up onto street level and sprinting north toward the park.

Michael was quick, but Lucille was even faster, so with her dragging him along, they ran so quickly they could not be seen by human eyes. They only stopped once they'd reached a spot in the park surrounded by trees where they weren't overlooked by anyone.

"What the hell was that? Those were the vampires we'd been looking for. They took Anna!" Michael protested.

Lucille just shook her head. "It's not so simple. Those

weren't ordinary vampires like you or me."

Michael frowned. They did look unusual, but still. They should have at least tried harder to rescue Anna.

"They're Soul Eaters." Lucille turned to face Michael. "They don't just drink blood, they drain their prey completely. Every kill makes them stronger, and over time, they've evolved into what they are now!"

What the hell was a Soul Eater? Why had he never heard the term before?

"So what? You're almost four-hundred years old, and I'm not a bad fighter either. Together we might have defeated them!" Michael argued.

"They would have torn us to shreds. Trust me." Lucille paced the clearing in the trees, back and forth, her arms folded. "Let me think."

Michael looked back in the direction where they'd just come from, but it didn't seem like they had been followed. Any vampire worth his salt would have caught up with them now, and if these two were really so strong, they wouldn't have had any trouble at all.

"So call more of your Council people. We'll defeat them with sheer numbers." Michael suggested.

"Still too risky."

"Well, we can't just do nothing. I'm sure Julius won't be happy if word gets around that anyone can just move to London and ignore the laws, whether they're Soul Eaters or not. It'll make him look weak," Michael said. The longer they waited, the more danger Anna would be in. If they had intended to kill her when they fed from her, they might want to finish the job now. If every mortal soul gave these monsters more strength, then what would happen if they took an immortal soul?

If they couldn't overpower them, then they had to trick them or outsmart them somehow. Although Julius was the wisest vampire Michael knew, he couldn't trust him to help if he didn't benefit from it somehow. Not after the incident with Cat…

That was it!

Michael took a deep breath and retrieved his phone from his pocket.

"What?" Lucille asked. "Have you thought of something? Who are you calling?"

"Alexander," Michael said.

Lucille's eyes widened. "Of course. Cat's blood!"

Michael smiled. They'd had a bit of a slow start, but throughout the night, Lucille and he had actually started to work as a team. The sparkle in her eyes told him she was on the same page.

"Hello, Alexander?" Michael started. This wasn't going to be an easy conversation, but it was unavoidable. Even Lucille seemed to agree on that.

"What's wrong?" Alexander asked, who must have picked up Michael's urgent tone.

"Those vampires who had left Anna for dead, they're so-called Soul Eaters."

"Ah." Alexander's reaction suggested he knew a lot

more about the topic than Michael did.

Lucille stepped forward and grabbed the phone from Michael's hand, switching it to speaker.

"Brother, they've taken the newborn," she said in a matter-of-fact tone.

Alexander sighed on the other end. "How many?"

"Two that we know of," Michael said. "We can't let them have Anna. They'll kill her!"

"Even with Council reinforcements…" Lucille started.

"Alexander, I need your help to get her back," Michael interjected.

"My friend, after what you've done for me last month… What do you need?" Alexander asked.

"We won't be able to defeat the Soul Eaters in direct combat, but if we had, say, a *secret weapon*…" Lucille said.

"Sister, you're not suggesting—"

"By all accounts, it ought to work. And she wouldn't need to be here. We could just use a little sample—" Lucille continued.

"I'm not ready to involve Catherine in this! The risk is too huge!"

"Just a few drops would do it," Michael said.

"Brother, you've got the most extensive library outside of the Council itself. Don't tell me you don't know what Soul Eaters are capable of. And to think we have two running wild around London? That's not just unacceptable, it's dangerous. Sooner or later, they'll catch wind of Catherine's identity and then, it might be too late.

Right now, we have the advantage."

Alexander kept quiet for a few moments.

"I can guarantee that this will do wonders for your relationship with Julius," Lucille added. "He'll take it as a sign of loyalty to his leadership."

Michael and Lucille exchanged a look. *He had to agree, right?* This was the only play they could reasonably make.

A rustle broke the silence on the other end. "I'll do it," Cat said.

"It's not safe," Alexander interrupted her.

"It never will be as long as Julius is angry with us. A little goodwill from his side could go a long way."

"Will you both hang on for a moment?" Alexander asked.

"Sure," Michael said.

He stared at the floor as the call went mute. Alexander and Cat had their own conflict to resolve. They'd made their case, and the matter was out of their hands now.

The line rustled again, making Michael perk up.

"Meet me at the house. I'll bring a sample of Catherine's blood. But after this, we'll be even, you understand?"

Michael breathed a sigh of relief. "Yes, Alexander. I understand."

"And dear sister, I need your assurances that you won't disclose the finer points of tonight's plan to Julius. If he thinks I'm handing out vials of Catherine's blood, he will want some for himself and that can't end well."

Lucille shook her head. "I won't say a word. I swear it."

"Thank you, my friend," Michael said.

The line went dead. Lucille and Michael shared a look.

"Thank you," he said.

She brushed his gratitude away. "I didn't do it for you. Imagine what will happen to me if it becomes known I've let a bunch of Soul Eaters run rampant under my watch. My position in the Council would be compromised."

Michael nodded. *Sure.* If that was how she wanted to play it, fine. He still didn't like Lucille very much as a person, but their partnership tonight had taught him that she was a powerful ally to have. Without her help, Anna would be doomed, and as a result, so would Michael.

He'd never planned to become someone's maker, but now that he was, he couldn't turn his back on her. If she didn't survive, he wouldn't be able to just shrug it off.

The Bond between them was too strong.

CHAPTER TWELVE

Michael and Lucille had returned home and waited in the library for Alexander to show up.

Michael sat in one of the two leather chairs as Lucille paced back and forth. Dawn was still hours away, but he grew more restless with every passing minute.

Finally, Alexander burst in, causing Michael to jump out of his chair.

"You made it. Let's go," Michael said.

Alexander gestured at him to sit back down. "Hang on. We must prepare ourselves, or we'll lose."

Michael pressed his lips together. Of course, mentors had a nasty habit of being right, and Alexander was no different. But the tightness in his chest hadn't let up all night, and he was at the end of his tether. *What if they were too late? How would he live with himself?*

"You brought the blood, yes?" Michael said. "What else do we need?"

Alexander approached one of the ceiling height bookcases that lined the wall. "It's here somewhere. Ah!" He reached up and retrieved a tatty old leather binder and brought it to the large mahogany desk that stood at the other end of the library.

Michael joined him and watched as he carefully unfolded the fragile documents inside to reveal plans and diagrams, hand-drawn on discolored paper.

"What are these?" Michael asked. "And how did you come by them?"

"Just an auction find. Never mind." Alexander inspected sheet after sheet until he paused on one marked 'Kensington.' "Here it is. These are plans from the 1920s and '30s, when they tried to streamline the London Underground system."

"We came across the two Soul Eaters in the sewer, though, not in a rail tunnel."

Alexander nodded. "It's all connected. Have a look here." He pointed at a section of tunnels marked in black ink. "These are part of the Underground network. Those dotted sections are part of the sewer. Was this roughly the spot where you had your confrontation with the Soul Eaters?"

Lucille leaned across the table and pointed out the exact location. "Here."

"Right. Well, if you look a little bit further north from there, there the two systems link up via a ventilation shaft."

"I could feel Anna's presence strongest over here." Michael pointed at a spot further south in the sewer line. Looking at the plans now, it made perfect sense. There was a dead end section of maintenance tunnel that crossed underneath the sewer. That was probably where they had imprisoned Anna.

"That's our target," Alexander said as he picked up the old plans and carefully folded them up again. "We'll have to create a diversion and then trap them once they turn up to investigate."

Lucille nodded and smiled. "The two of us can take of that, brother. They'll recognize me, and we can douse you in Cat's blood to disguise you as my prey. They won't be able to resist."

Michael straightened himself. "That'll give me the chance to slip into the other tunnel system from the ventilation shaft and get Anna."

"When is your backup coming?" Alexander asked Lucille.

"I can have them in position within a moment's notice. Then they'll capture the rogues at our signal."

"Good. Michael, you take this—" Alexander handed him a little vial. "Just in case."

Michael didn't need to open the small bottle to know what was in it. He nodded as they shared a look of understanding. It was deeply flattering that Alexander would trust him with a little sample of Cat's blood. Michael put it away deep in his pocket, fully expecting to return it to Alexander by the end of the night.

The three of them shared a look. It seemed like a solid plan. Certainly better than Michael's initial impulse of just heading down there by himself and fighting the two strange vampires to the death. With a bit of luck, they'd return home with Anna before long.

"I do believe we're ready," Alexander said. "Where are the weapons?"

Lucille gestured at him to follow her, but he stayed behind with Michael for a moment.

"It's going to be fine. Your woman will be fine."

Did Alexander just refer to Anna as 'his woman?' Michael frowned.

"Don't tell me you're still going to deny it?" Alexander asked, a coy smile playing on his lips. "Catherine was the first to notice it. Your expression when you talked about her gave it away."

Michael shook his head. "I'm her maker. That's all."

"I'll let you in on a little secret. Sure, there's a bond between maker and fledgling, and you would have sensed if she was in danger, but not like this. I can see you're in physical pain because of it. This something else, something deeper."

"That can't be. And it goes against everything—" Michael protested.

"Oh, hush! Deep down, you know I'm telling the truth. All that stands in your way is your misguided belief that your relationship is somehow inappropriate, when really, your situation is a lot more common than you'd think. Now let's go and get her back, or I will have potentially compromised Catherine's safety for nothing!" Alexander urged.

Michael pressed his lips together and swallowed, hard. Had he really been that far off the mark? Neither Alexander nor Lucille seemed to bat an eye at the chance of something more intimate developing between Michael and Anna. It would be so much easier to just let go of all the guilt he had developed since their one and only kiss. He took a deep breath and followed Alexander into the reception room, where Lucille waited with the weapons.

Fine. If they—especially Anna—made it out of this mess alive, he would confess his forbidden feelings to her. And then it would be up to her to decide how to move forward.

———◆———

It would have been easy for Anna to lose hope.

She'd been stuck in this dead end tunnel for hours, with nothing to keep her company but the periodic rumble originating from nearby Underground trains. She had become so used to the interval at which the trains passed that she'd started anticipating them.

Maybe a dozen or so trains ago, she'd felt some strange sensation, as though she wasn't entirely alone anymore. It was like she could feel Michael's presence, but that reassuring feeling had passed very quickly, leaving her alone again. Was this another one of those vampire sense things, like the one warning her of the rising sun? More likely she was starting to lose her mind already.

But if he did turn up, and Anna did get out of here, she would insist on a heart-to-heart with Michael. She would tell him that it was fine if he didn't want any sort of romantic relationship with her; she'd understand. They could just forget about the kiss and everything, and pretend it never happened.

The sad fact was that he was the only one she had now, and she couldn't bear for things to be awkward all the time. If they were going to be just friends, fine. They would never cross that line again.

Anna paced around her cell, investigating every inch of wall for the hundredth time, which only confirmed what she'd already known: she was trapped and there was no way out.

Then without any warning, the door to her cell swung open, revealing the creepy old vampire who had approached her out on the street.

She took a step back and bumped into the wall behind her.

Her captor smirked and seemed to float slowly in her direction. Could she make a run for it? Something told her he was only slowing things down in order to toy with her. He'd catch her without any problem if she tried anything.

"What do you want with me?" Anna asked.

He let out a chuckle. "Oh, dear child. How do I explain?"

By just telling me already, Anna thought. Her throat felt tight as her heartbeat sped up more and more.

He was only a couple of feet away from her now. "I am not one to leave unfinished business," he whispered, then leaned forward and inhaled deeply. "Ah. The smell of youth."

Anna kept her breaths and movements to a minimum.

She didn't want to provoke him. *Unfinished business?* They'd left her for dead, so was he going to finish the job now?

"Please don't kill me," Anna whispered. "Harming another vampire is against the law."

The man laughed. "Your innocence amuses me."

Anna frowned. She'd blurted it out without thinking. *So stupid.* If this guy cared one bit about Vampire Law, he might not have captured her the first time around.

"Then why not keep me around, if my presence amuses you?" she tried again.

He slowly shook his head. "I'm afraid that would be against *my* code."

Anna didn't dare ask what his code prescribed; she feared she already knew the answer.

"The male and the female who came snooping around. Acquaintances of yours?" the man asked.

Anna's heart jumped a few beats. So Michael *had* tried to find her already. She *had* felt him nearby.

"I don't know who you're talking about."

The vampire bared his teeth. If this was his way of trying to intimidate Anna, it was working.

"Don't play games."

Anna shook her head. "I swear, I don't know them."

"Do you swear on your life? On theirs?" he asked.

Anna pressed her lips together and averted her gaze. That was what she got for bluffing.

"As I suspected. Now, perhaps we can converse openly. I would very much like to learn more about these city dwellers."

What was the point?

"I really don't know very much about them," Anna said, which was much closer to the truth.

"Why did they save you? Were you their property?"

What a bizarre question. The way Michael, Lucille, and even Alexander seemed to live was quite different to the reality this strange vampire inhabited.

"No, they just don't kill humans." Anna frowned.

"Well, that's something new. Why wouldn't they kill humans? How do they gain strength?" The vampire moved around the dark cell, as though he was pacing, but his feet still didn't quite touch the ground.

"Are you certain they didn't keep you as a servant? I hear some Nightwalkers do that, enslave humans to run daytime errands."

Anna folded her arms. Perhaps she had said too much already. "Frankly, I don't remember much of my human life."

The old vampire smirked again as his deep black eyes focused on hers. "Of course you don't, child. I had made sure of that already."

So it was all *his* fault? The loss of memory hadn't been due to any injury or trauma, but hypnosis?

"Then why don't you undo whatever you did before, so that I may remember and answer your questions properly," Anna suggested.

Her captor paused and scratched his chin with white

spindly fingers. "I suppose there's no harm in trying."

Anna's heart beat a little faster again. Could it be so easy?

He grabbed her cheek, digging into her skin with long, claw-like fingernails. His eyes locked onto hers with a stare so intense she couldn't look away if she wanted to.

"Anything you had been made to forget, you shall remember it again."

Anna blinked involuntarily when she felt his presence enter her mind. It was unpleasant to have all this darkness, all this evil in her mind, but she could do nothing to defend herself.

She was frozen in place, unable to stir a single muscle or formulate any thought, beyond what he wanted her to.

Then, just like that, her mind was hers again.

"Well?" the vampire demanded. "What can you tell me about those two busybodies who came looking for you?"

Anna tried her best to answer his question, but she couldn't say a word. Her memories came rushing back, overwhelming her as she tried to process them. All of her old life: her worries, her fears, her ambitions and dreams.

She had wanted to run her own catering business, but when that didn't work, she'd gone back to work for her old boss. She'd picked up odd jobs, waitressing at parties and temping in restaurant kitchens. She'd worked sometimes two shifts a day, saving up money as well as knowledge.

She didn't have very many friends and certainly no boyfriends. The most intimate she'd gotten with anyone over the past couple of years had been that awkward kiss on the roof she'd shared with Michael.

Living in a modest single room in a house share allowed her to put as much of her earnings into savings as possible. Even if she made it out of here and went back there to pick up her belongings, she would end up with very little indeed.

She'd never achieved any of what she'd set out to.

"Tell me, or you'll regret it!" the vampire shouted.

She'd never really *lived*. And now she would die.

CHAPTER THIRTEEN

Michael was as ready as he would ever be. He waited in the shadows near the manhole from where Lucille and Alexander had already descended into the sewer. They were to perform their role in Anna's rescue—create a diversion—while he was going to wait here until the coast seemed clear enough to look for her.

From the moment Alexander had camouflaged himself with Cat's blood, Michael and Lucille had found it hard to resist the scent. These Soul Eaters would find it even more irresistible, since they were supposedly more bloodthirsty and guided by primal instincts.

As a result, Michael did not need to wait long.

Underneath him, a muffled commotion pierced the silent night. Footsteps fled north, just as planned; that would have been Lucille and Alexander. Something, presumably the Soul Eaters, chased after them, making more of a whoosh than the usual sound of footsteps he was expecting. Perhaps their increased power had afforded them the talent of levitation.

He waited for another minute or so, when he could no longer resist. As he was on his way down the manhole, the tension in his chest surged all of a sudden.

Anna was in very sudden, very real danger.

He ran through the sewer, ignoring the splashes of

dirty water landing all over his clothes, until he found the way through the ventilation shaft Alexander had pointed out on his old plans. From then on, the way was much drier and cleaner.

As he left the shaft and climbed into what seemed to be an old, now defunct part of the London Underground network, Michael paused to listen for any noises suggesting he'd been found out. Nothing. There was no movement anywhere around him, as far as he could tell. The tunnel ahead was empty, save for a few old signs abandoned on the ground.

He continued on much more slowly, trying to focus most of his energy on Anna. She was nearby, he could feel her so clearly.

Finally, he stopped in front of a heavy steel door with a crank handle in its center. Anna was in there, he would bet his life on it. He grabbed the crank, prepared to give his all to open it, when he found that it was already undone and the door opened with a simple push inward.

Inside, a pair of fearful eyes awaited. Anna.

Behind her stood a strange white-haired man Michael had never seen before. He looked even more bizarre than the two Soul Eaters they'd found in the sewer earlier that night. Older, more deformed, and more monstrous.

"Welcome, young one," the strange vampire said.

Anna tried to run toward him, but she couldn't move. One of the man's hands was on her throat, tightening visibly around her esophagus.

"Run," she whispered, barely able to make a sound.

Michael stood firm. He was not going to give up on her so easily.

"Run, dammit!" Anna repeated herself, her voice even more choked as the man squeezed her throat.

"She's cunning, this one. I like her." The man grinned, flashing his sharp teeth, then turned to gaze at Anna's neck. "Shame she must die. And once I've taken care of her, you'll be next."

Michael's entire body tensed up. No way. He would not let that happen. He slipped his hand into his right pocket and closed his fingers around the small vial Alexander had given him. Although he never expected to need it, he was glad to have it now. This would be his secret weapon, his only hope of defeating this ancient Soul Eater.

"You will do nothing of the sort," Michael said.

The strange vampire turned his head in Michael's direction again and glared at him. "You think you can stop me, young one? I am the embodiment of a thousand souls!"

"But that's my woman you're holding. I'm ready to fight." Michael glanced at Anna, who looked as surprised at his words as he was. They'd just slipped out before he had a chance to think things through properly.

"No matter, she's mine now. I finish what I start."

Michael stood firm with the bottle in his fist. Would Cat's blood be strong enough to disable the Soul Eater temporarily? Or would it just make him more violent?

Anna's position at the further end of the tunnel was less than ideal. But perhaps, if he threw the vial and broke it against the wall…

"Don't. He'll kill both of us," Anna whispered.

Michael looked into her eyes and all he could see was fear. The vampire turned to face Anna again, readying himself to drink.

This was Michael's last and only chance. He pulled the bottle out of his pocket and threw it as fast as he could against the back wall of the tunnel, smashing it into a million pieces and vaporizing the blood everywhere.

The Soul Eater's eyes turned red immediately as he turned his head to look for the source of the overwhelmingly delicious scent in the air.

Michael saw Anna, frozen in place, her throat now freed of the ancient vampire's grasp. She was shivering, her eyes deep red, as she tried to resist the urge to follow the blood herself.

Michael surged forward, holding his breath to minimize the effect of his diversion, and pulled Anna backward through the open door, slamming it shut behind them.

He turned the wheel as fast as he could, securing the bolts inside the door.

"Are you all right?" he asked, once he was done.

Anna was panting heavily, still shivering through her entire body.

"What. Was. That," she gasped.

"Blood. It's not important. He didn't hurt you, did he?"

She reached for her throat and swallowed a couple of times. "Not yet."

Her eyes turned their normal shade again, and she looked quite a bit weaker than before. Newborns needed more nourishment than mature vampires; she was probably due her next meal already.

"Let's get out of here, before that *thing* breaks out," Michael said, looking back at the door. It was so thick and heavy, hardly a noise filtered through. It seemed like the Soul Eater was still distracted by what little blood Michael had thrown against the wall.

"Sure," Anna said.

Michael watched her as they made it through the maze of tunnels and out into the fresh winter air. She remained quiet as they walked the streets, as though she was lost in thought, then suddenly paused at the next intersection.

"What is it?" Michael asked.

Anna pointed to the right. "There. That's where I lived."

"You remember? That's wonderful! Do you want to go pick up a few things?"

Anna stood frozen in place. For someone who had just unraveled the mystery of her recent past, she didn't seem even a little excited or pleased about it.

Michael continued to observe her. Why wasn't she happier? What was wrong?

She finally shook her head and started to walk away from the building she'd just pointed out. "There's nothing there for me anymore."

Michael frowned. "Wait! Don't you have anyone to say goodbye to, or personal items you want to take back to the house?"

Anna shook her head.

"I lived for my work. My biggest ambition was to run my own catering business. I'd even given it a try, as you might have figured out from the old business card we found. But I just didn't have what it takes, so I gave up everything—friends, relationships—and focused only on gaining experience and educating myself. I never succeeded." She sighed deeply. "It all seems so pointless now."

As Michael faced her, the sadness in her eyes nearly broke him.

"I don't know what I'm going to do now," Anna said.

He put his hand on her arm. "Remember up on the roof, that feeling of having the world at your feet? You can do anything. If you finally want to live that ambition of yours, you can do it so much better now."

Anna frowned. "I can? But I'm no longer human."

"You're faster, stronger, and smarter than you've ever been. And your senses are a hundred times more powerful than they were; you're now able to taste and smell things you would have never even noticed." He smiled nervously. "Do you think I would have lived in a mansion back when I was human? I was a bum who never amounted to much until I was turned."

"What about our limitations? I won't be able to go out during the day."

Michael brushed away her concerns. "Do what you can at night, and hire human staff to run errands during the day."

Anna turned and looked back at the street where she used to live, then turned and pointed at a cobbled street to their left. "There is something we can take back to the house."

"Tell me."

Anna shook her head. "It's best if I show you."

She waved at Michael and resolutely marched ahead until moments later, they stopped in front of a glass-fronted modern building that looked out of place among the Victorian and Edwardian buildings that surrounded it.

"These people make the best cinnamon rolls I've ever tasted," Anna said, gazing longingly at the switched off sign. "Do you think we could sneak in?"

Michael couldn't suppress a grin. Despite just having described herself as a rather serious workaholic, Anna did have a hidden wild streak.

"Listen," Michael said.

She did, and smiled when she heard it. "They're already at work inside."

Michael nodded. "While we absolutely will pick up some cinnamon rolls, it's time you had a very different sort of meal as well."

Anna's eyes widened. "I don't want to hurt anyone."

Michael shook his head. "You won't, I'll make sure of that. We'll take only as much blood as you need." He gestured at her to follow him, which she did, through a narrow alley that led to the backside of the bakery. They hid behind a large garbage bin and watched in silence.

A couple of men dressed all in white were in the midst of unloading a van full of raw ingredients. Anna and Michael gave them a few more minutes to complete the job, only then did they reveal themselves.

"Morning, lads," Michael spoke firmly, attracting their attention.

"Hey, this area is off limits!" one of the men protested.

Michael turned to Anna and nodded at her. "Hypnotize him. I know you have the talent."

Anna smiled briefly, then walked up to the man, whose demeanor changed immediately. Michael, meanwhile, invaded the other man's mind, rendering him harmless as well.

Then he stood back and watched in amusement as Anna compelled her subject to grab a box of cinnamon rolls from inside the bakery. As soon as he returned with their prize, Michael joined her and pointed out the right spot on the side of the man's neck.

"Bite him here. Drink. Count to five. Let go," he instructed.

Anna smiled nervously and took a deep breath. "Here goes nothing."

As it turned out, she need not have worried. Moments

later, they released the two men from their influence and watched as they went about their business without a single memory of what had just occurred.

CHAPTER FOURTEEN

What a night. Anna could not believe what all had happened in such a short time. Within a couple of days, her entire life had been turned upside down.

She slipped her hand into Michael's as they made their way back to the villa, so that soon after, they found themselves in exactly the same spot as the night before.

"It *is* beautiful here," Anna said, admiring the view of the house and its surrounding gardens, just as she had done last night.

Thanks to everything Michael had told her back in her old neighborhood, she had started to feel a bit more positive about the future. Perhaps she had gotten it all wrong; those old regrets were just that: old. They didn't matter anymore. Now that she had an eternity to look forward to, she could do whatever she liked.

Michael winked at her. "Race you to the top?"

Before she had the chance to agree, he was gone already. There was no way she could catch up, but she gave it her all and charged at the tree, climbed up the branches, and jumped up onto the house in record time.

Once she reached the roof, Anna found that Michael was already waiting for her with the box of cinnamon rolls in his hand. He gestured at her to sit down and opened the box, holding it in her direction.

She picked up one and inhaled deeply. Of all her old memories, it was this combination of scents which offered the most comfort; these were her guilty pleasure, her one indulgence in an otherwise lackluster existence.

"You really do love these cinnamon rolls, don't you?" Michael teased.

She opened her eyes and smiled. "Just try one. You'll understand."

He didn't, though, he just kept staring at her. His expression had turned from playful to completely solemn, which suddenly made Anna nervous.

"I should explain myself," he said.

She averted her gaze, letting it rest on Kensington Palace in the distance. This was where things had gotten awkward last night. "Look, if you just want to be friends, that's fine," she said.

Michael rested his hand on her arm. "I promised myself that I would tell you everything if we made it through the night in one piece. Suddenly I'm having trouble finding the right words."

Anna put the cinnamon roll back into the box and folded her hands in her lap, waiting for Michael to start talking. Whatever he was trying to say, it seemed important.

"I have always held the belief that the bond between maker and fledgling is sacred. That it is always meant to be platonic, more like a family relationship than anything else."

Anna's heart started to beat a little faster. So she had been right. He was trying to let her down easy.

"Then tonight, when it seemed like I might lose you forever, I achieved clarity. I made a terrible mistake, and I'm sorry."

Anna blinked a few times, trying her best not to feel awkward or hurt. She had prepared herself for exactly this conversation while she'd been locked up. So why did it now feel so wrong to hear him say these words?

"It's okay," she whispered.

"I'm not finished," Michael said, running his hand through his hair. "I was wrong trying to dismiss my feelings for you. You made me feel things I've never known."

Anna turned to face him. This wasn't what she thought he was going to say!

His eyes evaded hers and also focused on some spot further away in the park that lay in the distance.

"I couldn't bear the thought that something might happen to you, which is funny, since we've only just met." Michael glanced at her briefly. "I think… And if this is completely out of line, please do stop me. But I think I have come to love you."

Anna was stunned. She was expecting a lot of things, but not that. A declaration of love from Michael the supposed playboy vampire was the last thing she could have foreseen.

Her heart did a little happy dance inside her chest, even

if the entire situation was completely bizarre. Then again, over the last 48 hours, it had just been one bizarre event after another, so in a backward way, this development should actually make sense.

"I've also not felt like this, ever," she said.

His eyes locked onto hers. It was actually a bit funny seeing him this way. His demeanor since they'd first met had ranged from confident, to arrogant, to downright confusing, and she'd had trouble figuring out who he really was. But right now, she could tell that he had opened up. This was the real Michael, baring his vulnerabilities to her.

"So if you would forgive me for my strange behavior last night, I would very much like to start over," he said.

He was really rather cute like this. She pressed her lips together, but could not suppress a smile. "I would. I mean, I do. Let's start over."

She had only just finished speaking when he leaned forward, cupped her face, and pressed his lips against hers. It was magnificent, this do-over of their first kiss. Even with all of her memories restored, she still could not remember a time that she had ever felt so alive.

Her instincts had been right, he *did* care. He just had an incredibly crappy way of showing it. That was all going to change now, though; his confession promised as much.

Anna wrapped her arms around Michael, exploring him by touch and finally giving in to those illicit thoughts she'd been having about him. Their tongues danced around one another in a feverish frenzy. The fireworks she had felt the first time around paled in front of the pleasure his touch gave her now.

Before she knew what was happening, she found herself floating in his arms as they swiftly descended down the side of the roof and into a nearby window. Michael rushed her through the upstairs hallway, straight to one of the many bedrooms.

She briefly looked around only to note that she had never been in this room before. It must be his.

Now on her back on the bed, she watched as Michael unbuttoned his shirt. Was she ready for this? She'd thought of it after their first kiss and rejected the idea. *Not that kind of woman,* she'd said to herself.

All bets were off now. She wanted him. He wanted her.

What difference did it make who she had been in her mortal life? She was a vampire now. Powerful, strong, guided by instinct and pleasure.

She could have her cake and eat it too. And after getting to know Michael just a little bit, she was confident she would not be judged. The whole world lay at her feet now, as Michael had said. Anything she wanted, it would be hers for the taking.

Right now, all she wanted stood in front of her, only halfway done with the buttons on his shirt. *Too slow!*

She reached for him, almost clawing at the soft fabric. He understood, and with a naughty grin on his face, ripped it off in one swift move.

"Now do me," she demanded.

In the past, she might have felt insecure, but the way he was already looking at her, with lust darkening his normally light blue eyes, was all the reassurance she could wish for. He got onto all fours on top of her, leaned down, and grabbed the collar of her pullover with his teeth, then, without breaking eye contact, he tugged it off.

Anna gasped as the fabric split at the seams. How effortless it looked. Could she do the same? She pushed him back, fighting the barrage of goosebumps that spread over her naked skin as she felt his firm, chiseled chest underneath her hand. She would have plenty of opportunity to touch him. First, she wanted to play some more.

He stood back at the foot end of the bed, and she got down on her knees in front of him, pushing her fingers into the waist of his trousers and giving them a firm pull. They came off in shreds just as easily as her pullover had done.

This sort of strength she could get used to.

She dropped her own jeans and stood back, admiring him as he did the same to her.

They circled each other like animals prepping for a fight. It wasn't conflict they were after, though. Their end game would be so much more satisfying.

It was Anna who pounced first, jumping Michael and clinging onto him with her legs around his waist. They kissed again, more violently than before.

They had endless energy to spend, immense tension to

release.

Their bodies felt right together, hers slightly softer than his, but still more toned and powerful than she'd ever been before. Perhaps it was for the best that she was discovering all this with him to guide her. By now, she might have broken and bruised a human lover.

"You're beautiful," he whispered in her ear.

"Mhmm," she responded, as she nuzzled the crook of his neck and bared her teeth. Was this how vampires made love? She wasn't sure, just that it felt right.

He groaned, his low voice sending a shiver down her spine.

"You're tasty," she remarked, as she pulled back and licked her lips. She hadn't meant to hurt him, much.

His eyes narrowed and he grabbed her firmly by the back of her neck, guiding their lips together again.

"Let me see. Yes, that's rather nice, isn't it?" he mumbled, in between kisses.

Then, abruptly, he threw her off, back onto the bed, and approached on all fours again. His movements were smooth, deliberate, like a large feline stalking its prey. She felt her heart flutter as she waited for what he would do next.

He was on her within a split second, his weight pressing against her naked body, as his hand tore at her underwear. She was completely naked now, completely his.

Anna couldn't suppress a moan as his hard manhood pressed against her aroused sex. It was going to happen at last. She would discover just how extra sensitive all her senses had become.

When he entered her, she screamed. Along with all her past worries, her inhibitions had gone too.

He chuckled into her ear as he lowered himself into her. They became one. One pulsating, thrusting, moaning, and grinding mess of limbs.

The bed shook with every move of theirs, the paintings rattled on their fittings; even the chandelier in the center of the ceiling made its presence known in rhythmic jangles.

If this house had been any less solid, this furniture any more delicate, they might have destroyed it all. Not that Anna in particular cared much. All of this stuff was replaceable.

But this moment they shared now was priceless.

Her skin was tingly, on fire, and cool to the touch all at the same time. Every touch of his, every caress or squeeze, seemed to soothe her *and* send her nerves into an overwhelming overload of pleasure. She couldn't take it anymore, and she couldn't stop.

Then she felt it: the beginnings of her release. The pressure built and built until she could neither scream nor stay silent. Anna closed her eyes and dug her fingernails hard into Michael's back.

He never slowed or showed any sign of fatigue, he just kept going. The fireworks were back, bigger and brighter than ever before. What she saw behind closed lids was the perfect representation of her arousal as it built to bursting point. A volcano erupting, bright lights and fire everywhere.

She opened her eyes again and watched Michael as he closed his and groaned loudly, signaling his own release. It was like she could feel his pleasure as her own. She held him against her, admiring the smoothness of his skin with her fingertips.

"That was amazing," he whispered.

"It really was," she agreed.

What was even more amazing was that they had both orgasmed, and yet neither seemed tired at all. Dawn had not yet arrived; they still had time before they'd lose their energy.

Anna smiled subtly as she looked up at him.

He reciprocated and caressed the side of her face with the back of his hand.

"How about we do that again, and this time, I'll be on top?" she said.

His smile widened, exposing his fangs. "My thoughts exactly."

And that was exactly what they did, taking turns until the clock down the hall struck seven and Anna's body began to slow. The higher the sun rose outside, the duller their energy levels became. Finally, they ended up next to each other, with Michael's arm around Anna's shoulder, both sated and content.

Before she drifted off, Anna reflected once more on everything that had happened.

Just like that, she had gone from dejected and full of regret over the way she'd lived her human life to full of hope for the future. And she had found a lover to share this bright new future with, something that had eluded her during her human life.

Despite the twists and turns, everything had turned out all right.

CHAPTER FIFTEEN

It had only been one day since he'd confessed his true feelings to her. Michael turned his head and glanced at Anna, who lay beside him. His heart sped up at the sight of her.

One day down, eternity to go.

She was still sleeping peacefully, recouping from the excitement of the past few days. Being nearly killed by Soul Eaters, then turned into a vampire and captured by those same Soul Eaters again, had undoubtedly taken its toll.

Michael couldn't help but smile at her. How innocent she looked, resting with her eyes closed. Her calm expression was a stark contrast to the willful Anna he had come to know during the previous days. The one who was always ready to question her own reality, or him.

He realized now that he loved both versions of her equally. She would keep him on his toes. They would never have a dull moment together.

It was strange, how it felt like he'd known her for so long, when actually she had only come into his life a few days ago. To think that he'd tried to resist her charms at first seemed ludicrous now. He'd felt *guilty,* when the real tragedy would have been to let this opportunity get away.

For thirty years, he'd used this city as his playground. He'd seduced and courted numerous women, priding himself in his abilities as a conversationalist as well as a lover. But with Anna, everything had changed.

He was well out of his comfort zone with her. He couldn't just coast by on autopilot and expect that she wouldn't call him out on it. Being in a relationship was completely new to him. At the same time, her entire immortal life was still new to Anna.

They had so much to discover together; the possibilities were endless. Despite all his escapades, he'd never slept with another vampire before last night. It had been a revelation to share his body with an equal. But their connection had been so much deeper than just sex alone.

He was still her maker; he still felt responsible for her safety as well as her training as a new vampire. But added to that, he had new desires and hopes for her: that he could keep her happy. That she could live to her full potential and follow her dreams.

Whatever she wanted, he would be there to support her in every way he could. He hadn't told her this in so many words, but he would make sure to do that in time.

He carefully got up and stretched his stiff limbs.

"Where are you going? Don't leave," Anna whispered, her eyes still closed.

"I'm just getting something to eat. You stay here and rest," he said.

She did not respond; perhaps she had just talked in her sleep.

As he scanned the room for something to wear, he had

a sudden realization. Everything *was* new for them. But this place was old, and it wasn't even his. Perhaps it was time to take what had happened as a sign to make a few more changes in his life.

No longer would he live here in Alexander's shadow. The latter had Cat to take care of, whereas Michael now had Anna.

Getting something to eat now became second on his list of priorities. He grabbed a robe from the closet and retrieved his phone from his torn trousers on the floor.

Then he dialed Alexander's number as he quietly sneaked out of the room.

"Hope I'm not disturbing you. I was hoping we might have a chat, face-to-face," Michael said.

"I'm glad you came by, especially since you had to leave Cat alone in hiding." Michael glanced at Alexander, who had taken a seat in the armchair next to him in the library.

Alexander nodded. "No problem. Though let's not make a habit of it. I would very much like to move back into my house now that the main threat has passed."

Michael nodded. Fair enough. That tied in perfectly with what Michael wanted to discuss.

After his experiences with Anna, Michael felt like he understood his friend and mentor better too. He hadn't been able to relate when Alexander paired up with Cat and rebelled against Julius and the Vampire Council to protect her.

Now he understood things perfectly. He would do the same for Anna.

Still, he decided to broach the topic slowly.

"What's going to happen to the Soul Eaters?" Michael asked.

Alexander sighed. "They're Julius' problem now. Perhaps they'll be put to death for their crimes."

Michael brought his glass to his lips and savored the taste of the brandy as he swirled it around his mouth. Julius would have to take firm action; anything less would be seen as a sign of weakness by anyone looking to contest his leadership of the Council. Either way, Michael was glad he wouldn't have to deal with those two anymore and Anna would be safe.

"And the other human victims?" Michael wondered aloud.

"We were too late for them; they were probably killed even before you performed the Ritual on Anna. When we caught the two Soul Eaters down in the sewer, they bragged about disposing of the bodies in the river. Lucille will verify if they were telling the truth. Thankfully, she's quite a talented tracker."

"So I've noticed. I wouldn't even have known where to look for Anna without her."

Michael felt Alexander's eyes on him and turned his head to find his friend already grinning at him. "Don't tell me you and Lucille are friends now?"

Michael made a face. "I wouldn't go so far. But at least I know now that we *can* work together if necessary."

Alexander nodded, his expression still equally smug. "Whatever you say."

A few minutes passed in silence, giving Michael the chance to work up the courage to discuss the one thing he'd been holding back so far. His motives were pure, but he wasn't sure if Alexander would take it that way.

"I've been thinking," Michael began.

Alexander didn't speak; instead, he took a sip from his glass and waited.

"Perhaps it's time we move on—Anna and I."

Alexander frowned. "Whatever do you mean?"

"Well, it's not that I don't appreciate your hospitality, you know I do…" Michael also took a sip, not for courage as much as to buy some time to formulate himself properly. The last thing he wanted was to come across as ungrateful.

"But you want to leave?" Alexander asked.

"I just think it's for the best. Anna is still learning to control her urges, so I wouldn't want her to be a threat to Cat. We could also use some time alone together, to figure out how our lifetimes together are going to look."

Alexander's expression relaxed once more. He nodded in silence.

"You both will appreciate the extra privacy I'm sure. I know we will," Michael joked.

"Just know you'll always be welcome here, my friend,"

Alexander said.

"I do. Thank you. I probably wouldn't have lasted a decade without your guidance and help."

They shared a smile and raised their glasses.

"A toast. To immortality. And love," Michael said.

"And to family," Alexander added.

"To family."

They shared a little smile and each took a sip.

"I must say I wasn't expecting this, not yet," Alexander said. "Where are you going to go?"

"We'll stay in the city. Lucille tipped me off to some serviced apartments that would be perfect. And with the investments I've been making lately…"

"Anna's idea?" Alexander asked.

Michael shook his head. "I haven't even told her yet. But I have a feeling she will appreciate a place she can make her own. Figure out what this new life is going to mean for the two of us."

"It'll be an adjustment."

Michael wasn't sure if Alexander was talking about the two of them, or himself.

"Just don't be a stranger. And if you ever need anything…" Alexander's voice trailed off as he emptied his glass in one last sip.

"Thank you, my friend. Now, I'd better head back upstairs, see if Anna is up yet."

Alexander nodded and got up as well. They shared a short, if slightly awkward hug. "Any time."

***

ABOUT THE AUTHOR

———◆———

Dear Reader,

Thanks for reading Michael's Soul Mate. Although at the time I'm writing this it's not even a year since I released my debut series, Scottish Werebears, I'm not new to writing in general. In fact, my mom still tells me to this day about how I would make up stories, and attempt to record them in my clumsy, shaky handwriting from the moment I learned to read and write. From there I went on to write fan fiction and other stuff meant for my own eyes only.

I've always enjoyed stories of the paranormal. Vampires, shape shifters, witches and magic, all featured in the books I loved the most, even when I was still growing up. But it wasn't until much later that I got into romance. One of the first writers (a self published author just like me!) I came across was Tina Folsom, via her Scanguards Vampire series. I was hooked. From there I went on to read more paranormal romance until I found a new kind of hero I loved: bear shifters, like the kind written by Milly Taiden, Zoe Chant, and T.S. Joyce. What I love about bears is how they can be all strong and independent, a bit reclusive, and almost grumpy, but they always end up having a heart of gold (plus they tend to know their food, and we all know that a man who can cook is doubly sexy). All that (except for the shifting into a powerful bear) almost exactly describes the sort of man I ended up falling for and marrying in real life, so it's no surprise that this is what I started my publishing career with.

But no matter how many bear shifter books I've written, I've always longed to write a Vampire romance. Finally, once the Scottish Werebears series was complete, it was time to fulfill this dream with Alexander's Blood Bride (released in October 2016). And because I couldn't just stop at one, I immediately made plans for this follow-up. I hope you had as much fun reading it as I had writing it! By the way, book 3 has already been scheduled for February 2017, I do hope you'll join me for that one!

To find out more, check:

LoreleiMoone.com (And why not sign up for the newsletter to be the first to find out about new releases.)

You can also get in touch with me via Facebook (search for Lorelei Moone), or email at info@loreleimoone.com

x Lorelei

Michael's Soul Mate is the second book in the Vampires of London series. Although all books in this series are standalone and can be read out of order, perhaps you'd like to check out the story with which the series started…

About Alexander's Blood Bride

Cat has never been a social butterfly. The only reason she even agreed to go to the stupid Halloween party was because her friend and roommate Shelly wanted to attend. When she gets spooked upon almost falling into bed with the host, she's convinced it was all a big mistake. And what's worse, now people are stalking her wherever she goes!

Alexander Broderick has been hosting his annual Halloween parties for over a century. While his contemporaries use them as an excuse to engage in all kinds of debauchery, his own motives are more benign. He wants to converse, to get a feel for the times they live in through its people. But when Cat walks into his house, he forgets himself and is compelled to seduce her. There's only one problem: she's a so-called Blood Bride – a mortal woman whose blood smells so delicious that every vampire in town wants to drain her.

He knows he's the only one wanting to keep her safe, but can't act as long as she wants nothing to do with him. And then there's his own growing hunger to contend with. Can he protect her from the rest of the vampire community, as well as his own lethal cravings?

It's the ultimate forbidden romance; the love between a mortal and a vampire. What is it that makes flirting with death so utterly tempting? Read on and find out.

Buy a copy on Amazon (ISBN 9781913930288), or get more information on Lorelei Moone's website at loreleimoone.com.

SCOTTISH WEREBEARS

Did you know that Lorelei Moone started her career as an independent author with a whole series dedicated to bear shifters?

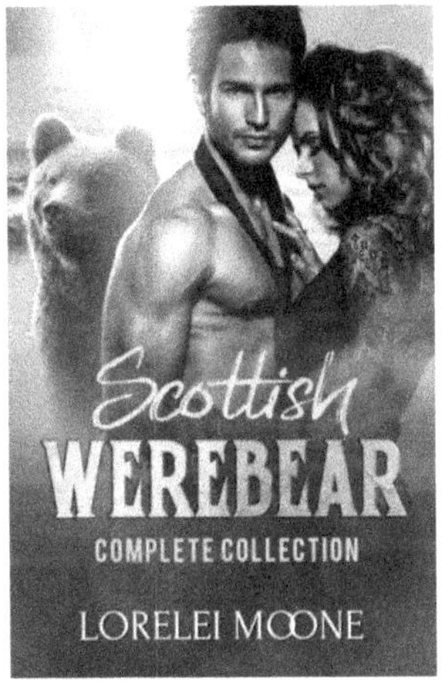

Check out the Scottish Werebears series, now available on all retailers. Book 1, Scottish Werebear: An Unexpected Affair can be downloaded for free in ebook format. All books are also available in paperback as well as audio.

About Scottish Werebear: An Unexpected Affair

Romance novelist, Clarice Adler, has lost the inspiration to write ever since dumping her cheating boyfriend. How do you dream up a plot of two people falling in love, when you've stopped believing in love yourself? But her deadline is looming, and her career hangs in the balance, so she decides to lock herself away on the secluded Scottish Isle of Skye to finish her manuscript. Upon meeting Derek McMillan there, it seems she's found her new muse and the words start to flow out of her as if by magic. Clarice falls for him, hard, despite knowing nothing about the man, except that he's unavailable.

Derek McMillan has been managing his farm and renting out a few holiday cottages on his own for years now. He deals with the occasional tourist for some extra money, but mostly keeps to himself. When he first lays eyes on the curvy beauty, Clarice, he immediately regrets accepting her booking. Lightning strikes, and as much as he tries to deny it, his inner bear knows that she's his mate. But he's a shifter, and she's a human, and the two can't ever mix, can they?

In this steamy paranormal romance novella, follow along as an impossible love blossoms between two people, who couldn't be more different. One might say fate intended for them to meet, if you believe in that sort of thing, but they're both set on fighting their attraction with everything they've got. They're going to need another push to admit to themselves as well as each other what's going on…

Please note that this is the first title in the Scottish Werebears Series. Each book features a different couple from first meeting to HEA, as well as an overarching external plot that won't be fully resolved until the end of the series.

Download your free copy of Scottish Werebear: An Unexpected Affair from your favorite ebook retailer, or get more information on Lorelei Moone's website at loreleimoone.com.